My Sister's Stalker

Nancy Springer

Holiday House / New York

To Jaime Fernando Pinto,
with love

Text copyright © 2012 by Nancy Springer
All Rights Reserved
HOLIDAY HOUSE is registered in the U.S. Patent and Trademark Office.
Printed and Bound in February 2012 at Maple Vail, York, PA, USA.
www.holidayhouse.com
First Edition
1   3   5   7   9   10   8   6   4   2

Library of Congress Cataloging-in-Publication Data

Springer, Nancy.
My sister's stalker / by Nancy Springer. — 1st ed.
p. cm.
Summary: When fifteen-year-old Rig, a loner, discovers that his popular
older sister is being stalked while away at college, he sets out save her, with
unexpected help from his divorced parents.
ISBN 978-0-8234-2358-3 (hardcover)
[1. Stalking—Fiction.   2. Brothers and sisters—Fiction.   3. Heroes—
Fiction.   4. Divorce—Fiction.]   I. Title.
PZ7.S76846My   2011
[Fic]—dc22
2010048645

oNE

At the time I had some qualifications to be a stalker myself, according to an FBI profile I read. I'm a guy—ninety percent of all stalkers are male—and I was a loner who could fit all his friends on the head of a pin. I can be obsessive, although I had no idea how obsessive; and I am more intelligent than average, although at the time I didn't know that, either, because I had low self-esteem, which is another characteristic of many stalkers.

However, I am *not* a sociopath. Nobody in my big-city high school cared about me, but I *do* care about people and what happens to them.

Even my sister. Okay, especially my sister.

Karma is four years older than I am, and the word *princess* comes to mind, yet she was my buddy right up until the family cataclysm. When we were young, she took care of me a little and played with me a lot. She was always Daddy's girl, so between that and being really involved in friends and school, she stayed with him after the divorce. I was, God help me, Mommy's little Riggie-Poo—Dad called me Big Rig because I wasn't—so I moved with Mom to a loft apartment in the city. And ever since then—well, you know how divorce makes a mess of everything.

Dad kept the house and stayed in Sumac, our hometown, so Karma could finish high school there. The last time I saw my sister was two years after the divorce at her high school graduation, where she was on stage nearly the whole time. She was senior class president, and one of the valedictorians; and she had been awarded a few hundred dollars' college scholarship for an essay she wrote, so she gave a thank-you speech. In my opinion, it's hard to look beautiful in a black cap and gown, but somehow Kari managed it, with her silver-blond hair streaming down around her face, a face that could light up a room.

Afterward we all posed for pictures together, and we all went out to dinner together, trying to act like a real family. I never missed Kari so much as when I was sitting right there at the table with her, but we could barely talk. I wanted to know whether she was dating, whether she was in love or ever had been, because I was thinking a lot about wanting a girlfriend, stuff like that. When we were kids, Kari and I used to tell each other everything. Well, almost everything. I wondered whether we still could talk that way. I wanted to know whether the divorce hurt her the way it did me. I wanted to know whether the smile she had flashed for the photos was as pasted-on as mine.

Another two years passed, so Kari was now a sophomore in college, and I was a sophomore in high school, definitely no longer Mommy's little Riggie-Poo. If people called me anything, they called me Rig. If they asked me what it was short for, I told them Rigmarole, because that was what my life felt like. (Try living with my mother.) I still wasn't as tall as most of the other boys, but I knew how to put a person down (a talent learned from my father), so nobody picked on me much. But nobody bothered with me much, either.

Including my own sister.

At first after the divorce, she tried to keep in touch, and so did I; but long distance, it's just not the same, you know? Then she kept getting busier, and now at college she was even farther away, like, in a different world. She had more to do than ever; and when we texted or talked, we didn't seem to be on the same page. She stopped phoning very often, which made me phone her even more, but mostly I left lame messages, and she didn't answer them.

It was one of those days. I had phoned Karma and asked her voice mail if she knew where the one-legged waitress worked (IHOP, get it?). Then, as if the food gods had heard me and disapproved, Mom had taken a creative notion and tried a new recipe for supper. With Mom it's either take-out or all-out. So we were eating this bizarre concoction she called Bohemian goulash, which consisted of something pale and stringy she said was parsnips, and likewise stringy pink stuff called rhubarb, and some squishy veggies, and a stringy squishy musky meat that was "real mutton," Mom told me proudly.

"Mutton?"

"Sheep."

"I'm eating a sheep?"

"The crowned heads of Europe have eaten mutton for centuries. You do like it, don't you, Ringgold?"

She's the only one who ever calls me by my real name. The fact that she named my sister Karma and me Ringgold, plus the Bohemian goulash, should give you a clue about Mom. She lives in a kind of fantasyland, which was not so great in Sumac but okay in the city, especially at the New Age art gallery where she works.

I ducked her question about the awful food by saying, "Mom, I've called Kari twice in the past week, and she doesn't answer."

"Of course not! She's a sorority girl. She's too busy having a wonderful time." Dreamily Mom looked over my shoulder at a Cinderella world that wasn't there. "Dresses, dances, boys falling in love with her."

Whenever Mom went over the top like that, it used to irritate the heck out of Kari.

I excused myself, heading for my bedroom and my computer.

Not admitting that I missed my sister, but anyway, I Googled her.

I typed *Karma Ebro* into the box, then clicked SEARCH.

Next moment, ranks of blue, underlined words lit up the white screen. "Karma Ebro" is for sure not a common name, so almost all of the listings were about her. Sumac Little Theater productions she'd taken part in. Facebook—been there, done that. Her sorority Web site, which I scanned for new photos and to check out her sister coeds, most of whom looked pretty good to me. She went to Fairview College. She was involved in student government again. Student council. And Fairview Community Orchestra—I found a picture of her playing her violin. And nursing homes she'd volunteered at, literacy programs, horseback riding for disabled kids, Habitat for Humanity—that was Kari, scheduled twenty-five hours a day trying to help the world. The list went off the page. I clicked NEXT.

Somebody's wedding—oh, she'd played violin in the quartet, which gave me another image to save to my pictures folder. "Karma Chameleon," Boy George, no good. Karma in Buddhism, *Karma* film, Karma yoga, no good. Ebro River in Spain, no good. KarmaEbro.net—what the heck?

Click.

KarmaEbro.net opened, and against a totally black background, I saw my sister. Top and center, her high school senior mug shot, which I happened to know she hated, for no reason I can see; she always looks gorgeous. Also her sorority portrait, then her Facebook photo, then photos from the Sumac H.S. junior prom and senior prom, and the time she was homecoming queen, and Kari with horse, Kari with violin, Kari with groups of friends, smiling at the camera.

Some of the pictures were from other Web sites, so seeing them again didn't bother me. But as I scrolled through pages of photos of my sister—eight, nine, ten—something nasty crawled into the pit of my gut and started bothering me plenty.

None of the photos were labeled. And in a lot of them, Kari wasn't even looking at the camera. It was like she didn't know somebody was taking her picture. She was maybe sitting in a classroom or walking down a street or coming out of a Walgreens or getting into her Jetta. The photos showed her looking in another direction or facing sideward or with her back turned. Some were from a high angle as if they'd been taken from an upstairs window or a rooftop, and others were from such a low level that this guy had to be lying on the ground or something.

Except—what made me think these were all taken by the same person, and that he was a guy?

My gut, that was what. A creepy feeling I couldn't quite name.

Who the hell had posted all these photos of my sister, anyway? There was no title on that black background, there was no explanation. There were no words at all. Just Kari after Kari after Kari, on and on until in the middle of a black screen they stopped. Then, centered at the bottom of the screen, there was a clip-art bouquet of red roses.

That didn't make me feel any better.

I sat and stared for a while before I backed up to the beginning of KarmaEbro.net and yelled, "Mom!" Kind of deluding myself that just this once she might act like a normal, helpful mother.

Actually I yelled, "Mom!" more than once. Several times over an interval of several minutes, until finally Mom came into my bedroom. "Ringgold, if you'd like to speak with me, I'd *much* prefer you would walk to my location rather than shouting."

"Yeah, I know." I couldn't explain why leaving the computer sitting there by itself would have felt like leaving the scene of a crime. "Mom, look at this."

"What? It's Karma!" Mom sounded pleased now. "Who put her on the computer?"

"I wish I knew. Here." I got up and motioned Mom to sit in my chair. "Keep looking. There's more."

She looked at the whole Web site, bubbling comments, like, "I helped her choose that gown!" "Where did she find that adorable sweater?" "These are from her Honors Club party!" "Do you have a copy of this photo?" I grunted uh-huh because

I didn't want to speak. Didn't trust my tone of voice. I wanted Mom to get it by herself.

Except she didn't.

She scrolled to the last page, the one with the bouquet of roses on it, looked at the photos and flowers, then just sat back and beamed. "Isn't that sweet," she said. "Riggie, your sister has a secret admirer."

And when she put it that way, I really wanted to believe her.

"I've never thought of the Internet as a romantic place, but this is *so* romantic," Mom said, looking up at me with a glow in her eyes.

I wanted to believe her because then I could feel okay again. I've lived with Mom all my life, obviously. I've seen her do some strange things, and amazingly, they almost always turn out okay. She acts like everybody is a good person. When we lived in the suburbs, Mom would hitchhike if she felt like it. Now we're in the city, and Mom will walk up to a guy who looks like a pimp and ask about the bus schedule. In two minutes she'll have him telling her the story of his life. Mom talks to strangers in elevators about her art, and they actually get interested and come to the gallery. Mom will talk to a drunk, a junkie, anyone; Mom hugs homeless people and doesn't get lice. She goes everywhere in the city, any time of day or night, and never gets mugged or has her purse snatched. Maybe it's because she's short and wide-eyed, and dresses in such mixed-up colors that in her Converse sneakers she looks like a forty-something child. Maybe it's because she flutters her eyelashes. I don't know. To her, everything is beautiful in its own way, and everyone is a friend just waiting to meet her. And somehow it works for her.

The truth is, I'd like to believe it works, period. Mom feels kind of like a religion to me, but I'm not sure about her. I'm like the dyslexic agnostic who wonders if there is a dog.

So Mom is also kind of a problem for me. I worry about her. I'd hoped she'd be a normal mom and worry about Kari, but she didn't.

"Oh, it's like Romeo and Juliet! Internet worship from afar. I have to call Karma right away!" Mom jumped up from my computer chair.

Quickly I said, "Um, I just tried. Her battery's dead." Which was a lie, but—my mistake for showing our mother—my stomach flipped at the idea of Karma hearing about this computer site from Mom, who would act like it was Boston cream pie when really it seemed more like mud. The best things about our mother were also sometimes the worst things.

"Oh. Oh, well. I'll get back to my cherubs, then." Mom makes these miniature 3-D worlds with bowers and ivory towers and princesses and trolls and things. This time it was baby angels playing in a water-lily pond. Watching her breeze out of my room, I hoped—actually I expected—she'd forget about Karma, because she is so, um, *attention deficit* I guess would be the polite way of putting it. I told myself that even if she did call Kari, probably she'd just get voice mail. I wondered whether Kari returned Mom's calls any more often than she did mine.

Kari. It had been so long since I'd really talked with her that I didn't know what to think. Maybe she already knew about the Web site, and she was okay with it? Maybe it was a joke? Maybe I was all creeped out about nothing? Maybe I just had a dirty mind?

Two

The next couple of days, all I could think about was that freaky Web site. I realized I *had* to find out who was following Kari around taking her picture, and why; like, whether it was as creepy as it seemed to me. I also had to find out how much Kari knew. She could be in danger of a Peeping Tom or something, you know? In my head I didn't want to take it much farther than that. It scared me. I wanted to tell Kari but not over the phone, especially since I didn't feel sure of myself. I mean, Mom said everything was okay, so maybe I was the sick one. Kid brother, raging hormones, and all that. I couldn't stop thinking, obsessing really, about my sister and the Web site and how I had no proof of any danger unless I could find out who was behind it. But I had no idea how to trace a Web site back to the person who had put it up.

I tried to think of somebody I knew personally who had that kind of computer skills, but there wasn't anyone. I needed help, but I didn't know who to ask. Police? There was nothing criminal about the Web site that I could see, and anyway, Karma's college was way out West—my sister knew how to *leave* home—so what could the city police do? I needed somebody who could give me advice. A teacher? Somebody at the art gallery? In my mind I went through all the adults I'd met since moving to the city, even the landlord, but I couldn't think of anybody.

Really, all the time in my heart I knew who I needed. I just couldn't quite face it.

So on the third morning after discovering the Web site, walking to school, all of a sudden I made a sharp right turn and started running. To the bus station.

I paid for my ticket, got on the bus, and waited for it to start rolling before I allowed myself to admit I was going to see Dad.

I knew better than to try just calling him. Whenever I phoned my father, he would greet me with, "Hey, Big Rig, how's it going in Artsyvilla?" which pretty much expressed his opinion of me and Mom and her work and her friends. But I like art and I can't help liking Mom, so my teeth would clench and it was hard to get words out. I would try to tell him stuff, but he barely listened because he was always multitasking. I could hear him keyboarding in the background. And in a few minutes, he would be ready to say bye and hang up.

Dad keeps his phone calls short, even at home, because he's always working. He's the boss of his own specialty-parts extrusion and milling firm, and he's a very busy man. He's at the mill about twelve hours a day, usually, and he really hates to be interrupted, so he probably wouldn't be glad to see me.

Two

The next couple of days, all I could think about was that freaky
Web site. I realized I *had* to find out who was following Kari
around taking her picture, and why; like, whether it was as
creepy as it seemed to me. I also had to find out how much Kari
knew. She could be in danger of a Peeping Tom or something, you
know? In my head I didn't want to take it much farther than that.
It scared me. I wanted to tell Kari but not over the phone, especially since I didn't feel sure of myself. I mean, Mom said everything was okay, so maybe I was the sick one. Kid brother, raging
hormones, and all that. I couldn't stop thinking, obsessing really,
about my sister and the Web site and how I had no proof of any
danger unless I could find out who was behind it. But I had no
idea how to trace a Web site back to the person who had put it up.

I tried to think of somebody I knew personally who had that
kind of computer skills, but there wasn't anyone. I needed help,
but I didn't know who to ask. Police? There was nothing criminal

about the Web site that I could see, and anyway, Karma's college was way out West—my sister knew how to *leave* home—so what could the city police do? I needed somebody who could give me advice. A teacher? Somebody at the art gallery? In my mind I went through all the adults I'd met since moving to the city, even the landlord, but I couldn't think of anybody.

Really, all the time in my heart I knew who I needed. I just couldn't quite face it.

So on the third morning after discovering the Web site, walking to school, all of a sudden I made a sharp right turn and started running. To the bus station.

I paid for my ticket, got on the bus, and waited for it to start rolling before I allowed myself to admit I was going to see Dad.

I knew better than to try just calling him. Whenever I phoned my father, he would greet me with, "Hey, Big Rig, how's it going in Artsyvilla?" which pretty much expressed his opinion of me and Mom and her work and her friends. But I like art and I can't help liking Mom, so my teeth would clench and it was hard to get words out. I would try to tell him stuff, but he barely listened because he was always multitasking. I could hear him keyboarding in the background. And in a few minutes, he would be ready to say bye and hang up.

Dad keeps his phone calls short, even at home, because he's always working. He's the boss of his own specialty-parts extrusion and milling firm, and he's a very busy man. He's at the mill about twelve hours a day, usually, and he really hates to be interrupted, so he probably wouldn't be glad to see me.

Mom was not going to be thrilled with me, either, for taking off without telling her.

I got out my cell phone and texted Mom, *gon 2 c dad*; then turned it off to postpone the reaction. Mom's habitual happiness would be violated. I'd never skipped school before, much less caught a bus back home to Sumac. Heck, I'd never visited my father except on holidays, which was obligatory. The rest of the time I tried to stay away from him. He doesn't like my hair, my clothes, my posture, my looks, my warped sense of humor, my interests—altogether I'm a disappointment to him. I wasn't looking forward to talking with him.

But there I was, getting off the bus and walking the few blocks to his office building, feeling really weird being back in the town where I'd lived until I was twelve. Not much had changed except me. Now in the city I was nobody, but back then in small-town Sumac I had been somebody, sort of, because my father employed half the other kids' parents. I've never understood what his business really makes or does, but Dad's always analyzing efficiency studies and sales figures and stuff. His paperwork usually took him all morning, and it wasn't noon yet, so good. I saw his Mercedes parked in its Director Only space, so I knew he was in. I'd probably find him at his desk.

I felt stressed-out numb, not knowing what kind of welcome I'd get. I could have called to tell I was on the way, but for some reason it was very important for me to just walk in and check out the look on his face.

His secretary's jaw dropped when she saw me heading across the thick green carpet. But before she could reach for the intercom, I put a finger to my lips, like, shhh, it's a surprise, and she smiled. I went to Dad's door and knocked.

"Who is it?" he yelled, his tone slightly irritated, I guess because his secretary was supposed to intercept people.

I took a deep breath and opened the door.

Glancing up from behind his big desk, he dropped the papers he was holding and elevated out of his chair. "Riggie!" I'd never seen him so surprised and, yeah, maybe even glad—for a nanosecond. Then he frowned. "What are you doing here? Why didn't you tell me you were coming? For God's sake, stand up straight. Why do you kids wear those huge, grotesque shoes?" In his usual wing-tip shoes to go with his usual three-piece suit, he strode around the desk and patted me on the back a little too hard. "Today's no good. I have to meet an important client for lunch in ten minutes. If you had given me a couple of days' notice—"

"I didn't know I was coming until I came."

My voice sounded weird even to me. Dad stopped where he was, took a good look at my face, and frowned harder. "Are you having problems with your mother?"

"No, not really. I—"

"Kids in school picking on you? You've got to learn to stand up for yourself, son."

"I have to show you something on the computer."

"What? Now? I don't have time."

But I was already at his computer, clicking away with the mouse.

"Rig, I only have"—Dad glanced at his Rolex—"eight minutes."

That was all right with me. It took me less than one minute

to bring up KarmaEbro.net, and then I just stood aside and gestured for him to sit and look.

He sat. He scrolled through the photos. Partway through, about the sixth page, he turned away to buzz his secretary on the intercom. His voice sounded stretched out of shape, kind of like mine. "Julie, call today's lunch and tell him I can't make it. Family emergency—No, don't say that, people ask questions. Just tell him I feel like I might have the flu. And hold my calls. And Julie, not a word to the gossip mill about anything you see in here today." The way he said those last words let both me and Julie know she'd be fired if she blabbed.

Then he turned back to the computer and kept looking at pictures of Karma. In a low voice he asked, "How did you find out about this, Rig?"

"I Googled my sister." With Dad it's no use going into full explanations.

"When?"

"Sunday night."

"And today's Wednesday." He sounded grim. "Why didn't you call me at once?"

"I wasn't sure. Mom just thought it was romantic, and they say teenage boys are so preoccupied with sex it comes to mind every eight minutes on the average, and I'm no exception, so I thought maybe it was just me."

Dad was giving me the annoyed, uncomprehending look that usually results whenever I forget it's no use going into full explanations. "You showed this to your mother?"

But I barely heard the question. I gasped and lunged toward the computer. "Those weren't there before!" I pointed to three photos at the bottom of the—gallery, I guess you could call it. Photos of Kari at her desk with her laptop; Kari sprawled on a single bed, studying; and Kari still on the bed with her books, but sleeping. "He's added those since I saw it before!"

Dad looked up at me. "Are you sure?"

"Yes! I mean, I'd remember!" My voice shot up into a squeak; I hate that. "He must have taken those through her window at the sorority house."

"What have you told your sister?"

"Nothing! She doesn't return my calls!"

"Mine either," Dad said more softly.

He sat in the computer chair. I stood marooned in the middle of his plush carpet. We stared at each other. For once we both seemed equally lost.

I spoke first. "Dad, you've been to Kari's college, and I haven't. Were those last three pictures taken through her bedroom window?"

"I think so, yes."

"Then in three days the creep's gone from sneaking around after her to standing right outside her room."

He didn't ask me what creep or what I was talking about. He just turned around and buzzed his secretary. "Julie, get me the file on Fairview College."

I didn't ask him what he was going to do. I knew better. Dad's like the general in the army; you don't question him. But he did mutter, mostly to himself, "First thing is to inform campus police."

I burst out, "Dad, for all we know it *is* somebody in the campus police. I mean, any nut can be a rent-a-cop."

"Well, what the heck do *you* think I should do, then?"

"There's got to be some way to trace the Web site. See who's posting it."

He stared at me a moment, then nodded, reached for a white phone, pressed a button, and waited only a second before he said, "Wally? George here. I have a problem with my office computer, and I need somebody very smart and also *very discreet* to handle it. Could you—"

He didn't need to finish the sentence. He nodded, said thanks, and hung up.

All of a sudden I felt sick. Like, God, Kari really was in danger, and I'd made a big mistake not telling Dad sooner. But also it was like, now that Dad was in charge of the boat, I could go ahead and be seasick and throw up. I tried to look at Dad, but he was out of focus.

"Rig!" He jumped up and caught me just as I was about to fall. "Sit down." He helped me to a chair. As he said, "Head between your knees," his strong hand pushed it there.

He let go, and I sat with my head down, feeling wobbly in a different, slightly better way because he was taking care of me, yet despising myself for being weak.

Dad shoved a glass of what looked like golden water into my hands. I took a sip and almost choked, but I felt less shaky right away. I sat up.

Dad nodded at me. The door opened, Julie came in with a file folder, and as Dad took it from her, he asked me, "Did you eat yet today?"

Eat? I'd been too worried to eat breakfast. I shook my head.

"Order in sandwiches, Julie, and some Coke or something."

After the secretary went out, Dad looked at the drink in my hand and said, "I could use one, too."

"What is it? Brandy?"

"I wish I had brandy. No, it's whiskey." He poured himself a little in a glass, took a sip, shook his head, and told me, "You'd better not drink any more. I don't want to corrupt the morals of a minor."

I didn't understand him any better than he understood me. I just mumbled, "Sorry," feeling really embarrassed because I'd almost barfed or fainted or both.

"Sorry? What for? Don't bother. No time." Dad sat down at his desk, flipped open the folder his secretary had brought him, and phoned Fairview College.

THREE

I don't remember everything he said or how many people he talked to, partly because I was trying to do some things on my own so as not to feel completely useless, and partly because Dad's tone of voice scared me. When he wants people to pay attention, he uses his voice like—I don't know, like the dark music in an old movie. I've always felt scared of him when he talks that way, even when he isn't talking to me. He laid all his dark tone on the phone, the gist being that he had reason to think his daughter was in danger. He wanted the full cooperation of the campus police, but before that he wanted Karma located. He wanted somebody to look at her class schedule and track her down; he wanted her paged in the library and the student center; he wanted someone to check with her sorority, issue a campus-wide memo, call campus security; do whatever it took to locate her and get her to call him *now*, if not sooner.

Meanwhile, I texted her, *sis call me*, and then I sat in the computer chair and started printing out all the KarmaEbro.net pictures one by one. I wanted to see whether any of them were print-protected in any way. They weren't, so we couldn't trace a copyright. That was part of my idea for printing them out. The other part of my idea I barely knew myself yet.

About the time I finished, Julie brought in a bag of Subway sandwiches and a cardboard holder of drinks. She had to wonder what was going on, but she didn't even look around the office, just set the things on a little circular table, got out a couple of folding chairs, and served lunch as if she were a waitress.

Right after her, in came a skinny guy in a suit and tie who waited until Dad looked at him before he said, "Wally sent me." He was the very discreet computer expert.

Dad nodded at him. "You will say nothing, ever, to anyone, about anything you see in this office today." Which I guess included me, but Dad pointed the man toward the computer. "It has come to my attention that someone seems to be stalking my daughter."

The word hit my chest like a minor heart attack. My father had said it. The s-word. *Stalk. Stalking. Stalker.*

It made me shaky again. Dad glanced at me—I was standing at the printer, waiting for the last few pictures—and said, "For God's sake, Riggie, eat something."

Eat. Yes. Quick. I sat at the food table and shoved an Italian sub into my mouth. It was probably a good sub, but I wouldn't know. I forced it down bite by bite as if I were eating medicine.

Meanwhile the computer guy settled in and looked through KarmaEbro.net. "Very disturbing, sir," he told my father, "and very clever. Nothing to identify himself, no overt threats, no overt sexual content. Nothing to call the police on."

"I'm going to call them anyway." Dad sounded grim, reaching for his drink. "Meanwhile, is there some way you can trace that site for me?"

"I can trace the TCP/IP number of the computer that generated it."

"Do that. But what about the *person* who generated it?"

"Whoever has access to that particular computer. There's a database that allows me to locate the origin to a general area geographically—"

"We already *know* the area geographically!" Dad exploded. "It's where my daughter goes to college. Can't you find out *who* put that—that—"

"Crud," I offered, as words seemed to have failed him.

"I wish I could think of a stronger term without insulting Kari."

Just then the phone rang. He snatched it up. Please, it had to be Karma.

It wasn't. I saw my dad's face sag as he said, "Hello, Rosalie."

Aaaak! My mom. From clear across the room I could hear her, shrill and upset, talking nineteen words to the dozen, as my grandfather used to say. Not for the first time, I wondered why in the world my mother and my father had ever married. I guess opposites really do attract.

Dad cut in. "He came to inform me someone's stalking Kari. . . . No, we're not overreacting!" Although in a way I guess we were. Both of us were so scared of what might happen to Karma that we felt like it had already happened. We were reacting to an emergency that hadn't taken place yet. Dad continued, "Yes, your son is right here. *Our* son. He's quite safe. I promise

I will buy him a toothbrush, and no, you can't speak to him because I need to keep the lines open.... I have no idea. We'll keep you informed. *Good-bye*, Rosalie."

After Dad hung up, he swiveled in his desk chair to peer at me, but he didn't say anything.

"No idea of what?" I asked after we had listened to the computer expert clattering on the keyboard for too long.

"No idea when you'll be going back. I consider that you uncovered this problem, and you deserve to see it through."

Unbelievable. My dad didn't want to get rid of me. I took another bite of the Italian sub, and it tasted pretty good.

A couple of hours later, Karma still hadn't called. The computer guy had given Dad the stalker's TCP/IP number, for what it was worth, reaffirmed that he would tell no one about any of this, then left since there wasn't anything else he could do. I was on the computer researching the relevant topic. Dad was alternately on the phone or sitting in his desk chair, breathing deeply and squeezing a stress ball in each hand.

"Dad," I said to him during one of these lulls, "it says here that only two percent of stalkers escalate from watching and fantasizing to actually harming their targets."

"Ninety-seven percent of all statistics are invented," he muttered, but he got up and leaned on my chair, reading over my shoulder. "It says that they slash tires, invade homes, steal underwear, leave dead rats on the bed."

"Only after they flip over to the hate side of their love/hate complex. They're obsessive and won't take no for an answer, but our stalker is still sending roses, not dead rats. At least online."

The phone rang. Dad got to it in three steps. But it was some private detective returning his call, not Karma.

"Yes," Dad explained, "I want someone to go to my daughter's college campus, find out who is stalking her, and put a stop to it. Are you qualified?"

He listened and asked questions, but I could tell he was not satisfied. He hung up quietly, sat for a moment, then buzzed his secretary.

"Julie," he told her, "call Sumac International Airport." That was a joke; Sumac had no airport except the little place out by the quarry. "Charter us a flight to Fairview. Yes, the closest municipal airport. Yes, today. Now."

FoUR

Sumac "International" really was a *little* airport—no airlines or commercial flights, just bright-colored baby airplanes that people flew for a hobby, I guess. The one Julie had chartered for us was orange and blue, and had two propellers. It could fly six people if they were skinny, but Dad and I between us pretty much filled the back of it, what with his briefcase, my bag of sub sandwiches, and, Dad complained, my feet. "Would you please park them out of the way?"

"I can parallel park the Nikes under the seat if you can stand the smell of my socks." I didn't usually say things like that to my dad. But by now it was four o'clock in the afternoon, Karma still hadn't called, I was going to fly in a small plane, which I had never done before, and altogether I was feeling kind of loopy.

"God, not that. Anything but the smell of your socks," Dad said. I couldn't figure out the look he gave me before he leaned forward to talk to the pilot. "It is absolutely vital that I keep my cell phone turned on." He had rigged it so his office calls would forward to his cell.

"And that is absolutely no problem, sir."

"Will we be there before dark?"

The pilot was a young guy, fitting his earphones over his baseball cap. "If this nice tailwind keeps up, yes, we should."

I was too fogged with worry about Karma to enjoy the takeoff much, or spend much time looking at the bright autumn view below, mazy housing developments dotted with yellow maples. I had my photo printouts in the plastic bag with the sandwiches, and I took them out and started messing with them. I tried to put them in chronological order, based on season of the year, clothing, that sort of thing. Then I tried to figure out which ones were taken in what places, making piles on the seat. After that I started to sort them into, let's face it, leg shots, butt shots, boob shots, whatever, although it hurt my gut to think of my sister that way. But I gave it up pretty quick. I had a feeling Dad wouldn't like it if he knew what I was doing, which he didn't. For the past hour he had been leaning back with his Bose headset on and his eyes closed.

But he jumped like popcorn when the cell phone rang. Not his. Mine.

I flipped it open, saw Kari's number on the screen, and started grinning like a pumpkin head as I spoke into it. "So *now* you call your kid brother."

Her unmistakable voice complained, "I can't help it I'm busy! I've been studying..."

Dad leaned toward me, pop-eyed. I gave him a thumbs-up. He closed his eyes and sank back in his seat.

"...the old Indian mound in the middle of the graveyard all

day," Kari was saying, "and I get back to campus, and every-body's looking for me." Her voice is kind of the color of her hair. "Riggie, I don't want to call Dad back till I get a clue. Is it a family crisis or something? Do you happen to know why he practically put out an APB on me?"

"Yes, I do know, but hold on a minute. Kari, where are you right now?"

"Standing in the middle of the quad! Why?"

"With people around?"

"Of course! What—"

"There's a possibility you might be in some danger."

"This is one of your lame jokes, right?"

Dad leaned forward and gestured for me to give him the phone. I fended him off with a raised first finger—one minute. "No. It's not a joke. That's the bad news. But listen, the good news is, there's no need for you to phone Dad."

"Huh?"

Grinning, I passed the phone to our father, making sure I switched the speaker on first.

"Kari, I'm right here," he said, "and I've never been so glad to hear your voice." His own voice was not quite behaving for him. He had to clear his throat before saying, gruffly, "Riggie and I will be there in a few minutes—"

"What?" I could hear her even through all the airplane noise.

"Do you know where the Fairview Airport is?"

My sister is a very intelligent person, but the concept that Dad and I were together, sharing the same space, stunned her so much that it took her several moments to grasp the nature of that space.

"You're where?" she gasped.

"A few miles over your head."

"In an *airplane?*"

"One should hope so."

"But—but what's going on?"

"Nothing, I hope. I *very much* hope this is all about nothing at all. Now, Kari, pay attention. Can you meet us at the airstrip, or should we hire a car?"

She met us. We saw her white Jetta pulling in as we landed, and we just walked off the plane across the pavement and through a gate as she came running toward us across the parking lot—how girls can run in clogs I'll never understand—and it was like she'd just come back from Iraq or something, except we were the ones getting off the plane. Anyway, we all met in a three-way bear hug so warm I felt like a lightbulb.

Kari was the first one who pulled back. "You're scaring me," she said, even though her face was still shining with her smile, "the pair of you, not just coming here but coming here *together.* What in the world is going on?"

Dad said, "Um..."

"Is Mom okay?"

"Yes! Yes, your mother's just as usual."

"Then what *is* the 'nothing' that this fuss is so-o-o-oo all about?"

Dad said, "I, uh..."

"Kari, do you have your laptop in your car?" I asked.

But she was looking at the terminal and the twin-engine airplane taxiing away. She asked, "Don't you have any baggage you need to grab?"

"No," said Dad in owlish tones. "I promised your mother I

would purchase a toothbrush for Riggie. And I intend to honor that promise."

"You're goofy," Karma declared. "Would you please tell me what is going on?"

"Laptop?" I hinted.

Yes, she did have it in the Jetta. She'd been out all day at an Indian mound, lying in the grass in a T-shirt and blue jeans, trying to get some schoolwork done away from other people, and now her computer was plugged into the car's cigarette lighter to recharge. With Karma in the driver's seat, me in the passenger seat, and Dad looming over both of us from the back, I did my thing, KarmaEbro.net, then passed the computer to my sister.

As she took it in, page by page, neither Dad nor I said a word. But I watched Kari, and even though she never looked at me, I saw how it seeped into her like something intravenous and toxic, gradually turning her from relaxed to rigid, almost paralyzed.

"Sick," she whispered when she got to the end. She might have been commenting on the Web site. She might have been saying how she felt.

Dad waited for her to take several deep breaths before he asked quietly, "Any idea who?"

She shook her head.

Remembering my research on stalkers, I asked, "Anybody you keep running into, like, he always seems to be there?"

"Not that I've noticed. I mean, sure, I see the same people all the time, but it's a small campus."

"Anybody who stands and stares at you?"

"No," she replied between her teeth, and as she booted down and closed the computer, I noticed her hands were shaking. I looked at her face and realized her shock was flaring into anger. Her blue-green eyes narrowed and blazed. Sounding a bit like Dad, too quietly, she said, "This isn't fair. Some pervert is following me. What am I supposed to do, look over my shoulder all the time? Lock myself in my room? Wear a Kevlar vest, a bike helmet, maybe a chastity belt?"

"Yeah, where do we get one of those?" I asked.

Karma shot me a dirty look.

Dad said, "The first thing we need to do is get the cooperation of the local police."

The occupants of the Fairview PD were not thrilled to see any of us, and basically let us know there was nothing they could do about my sister's stalker until he did something to her besides take her picture. This was not the reaction Dad wanted. At the very least he expected police protection, stepped-up patrols, an investigation. He demanded to see the top cop; and while Karma and I waited on a bench in the hall, we could hear him using his voice like a Wagner symphony to impress upon the man the importance of George Ebro and his daughter.

Kari leaned back with her eyes closed. "I cannot believe any of this is happening," she muttered.

"I know what you mean. I took me three days to go to Dad."

She opened her eyes and turned her head to stare at me. "You went to Dad?"

"Well, I had to. Mom wouldn't take it seriously. She's all warm and fuzzy like you've got a sweetheart."

"Blech." Kari was still staring. "Dad didn't send you straight back to Mom?"

"No! It's like he actually wants me around. Go figure." It had been a very long day, but somehow my wiped-out brain managed to burp a question I needed to ask her. "Sis, when did you change your hair?"

"Huh?"

"Now it all hangs down, but you used to have this fringe across your forehead—"

"That's called bangs, doofus."

"Why? Does something go 'bang'?"

She rolled her eyes. "It's just a *word*. I grew them out the summer between high school and college. Why?"

I didn't answer, just pulled the papers out of my plastic bag and started sorting them into two piles, Karma with bangs and Karma without bangs.

"My ugly mug shot was in the Sumac so-called *News-Herald*," she said, irritated. "So were some of the others. Anybody could get them online."

"This one?" A picture of her with friends at a party.

"Kids made copies. Maybe somebody put it on Facebook."

"What about—"

But before I got a chance to show her any more pix, Dad rammed out of the office, scowling. Obviously he had not managed to tell the top cop what to do. "Come on," he ordered, striding toward the front door. I just had time to scoop my pictures together and follow.

When he was in that kind of mood, I didn't dare speak to him, but Karma did. "Dinner, Dad." she suggested gently. "I am a starving college student. Feed me."

FIVE

Feed the starving college student, yeah, right. Karma doesn't like red meat, but she drove us straight to the best steak house in town. She knows Dad. Once he had ordered his T-bone and was settled in with a draft lager, we could practically have measured the static slowly discharging from him. Neither of us tried to talk to him, but Karma asked me, "Riggie, how's it going in school?"

I made a so-so gesture with my hand.

"What's that mean?"

I shrugged. "It's a city school. Course offerings out the woz. I could take Phoenician archaeology if I wanted to. But it's hard to make friends."

Kari, who has never in her life found it hard to make friends, looked puzzled. "How come?"

It felt so good to have her attention that I really tried to answer. "When I moved there, sixth grade, all the cliques had already clicked, you know? Plus, it's a big city, so you don't just happen to meet anybody outside of school. And—"

"If you would only make an effort to get involved," Dad growled, "the way I keep telling you—"

Kari interrupted him sweetly. "Daddy, don't start."

I said, "I've joined some stuff. Library volunteers, tutoring." I stopped short of mentioning art club. Dad has no use for art.

"Art club?" Kari asked.

What was she, psychic? Without looking at Dad I told her, "Sure, but it's no good. It's like I don't know how to make new friends. Before the divorce I just ran with the same bunch of kids since preschool."

Which is how we ended up talking about the divorce even after the steaks (and Kari's shrimp scampi) had arrived. Partly because Mom wasn't there to make us pretend everything was perfect. And partly because, if we hadn't talked about the divorce, we would have had to talk about the stalker, which was worse. So even Dad opened up a little. "It wasn't anybody's fault," he said. "I didn't have a mistress, your Mom didn't have a lover, nothing like that. It was just—your mom was so cute, like a child, when I met her. . . ."

"Still is," I said.

"Whereas I was born a grouchy old man."

"And you still are," Karma told him affectionately.

Dad's smile wasn't grouchy at all. "There's a reason opposites attract. It makes multitalented children, so it's good for the species. And your mom and I were good for each other at first."

"But you were so different, all that friction, it wore thin, right?" Karma suggested.

"Well, struggling to make it in business, and pay the mortgage, and then..."

"I notice you're trying very hard not to blame us kids," said Karma.

"There's no blame! When we had children, I wanted her to grow up and be a somewhat normal mother, that's all. My mistake."

"And she wanted you to mellow out," I put in.

This was what I wanted, too, and he knew it, so there was a tense silence.

"Anyhow, we got to a tipping point when your mother wanted her own life in Artsyvilla," my dad went on with minimal sarcasm. "And I can't say I was thrilled, but I don't hold it against her. She is who she is."

"The Tao of Dad," I said, actually meaning it as a compliment, although I'm not sure how he took it. "Speaking of Mom, I ought to phone her. Do you want me to leave the table?" There had been a lot of tension during the divorce, no matter what he said now.

He stiffened but told me, "What for? I'm a big boy. Give her a jingle."

I tried the land line—Mom may be one of the few people in the city who still has a home phone—and she picked up right away. When she heard my voice, she had a good bit to say about how upset she'd been, the school had called her to ask where I was, why in the world had I gone off without telling her, et cetera. Once she took a breath, I cut in.

"Mom, guess what. Dad and I are in Fairview, having dinner with Karma."

"Are you getting along all right with your father?"

"You're supposed to worry about Kari, not me."

"You know I think it's silly to worry. But if your father wants to spend his time and money, that's his business. How is Karma?"

"Supremely drop-dead gorgeous, as usual." Quite the opposite of her dweeby brother, moi. "Crowned with her usual invisible tiara." Hand in the air, Kari was threatening to smack me. "You want to talk to her?" I shoved the phone into Karma's uplifted hand, grinning at the look she gave me.

"Hi, Mom.... Sorry, I've been so busy I didn't even go to homecoming.... Yes, I've seen it. No, I don't think it's a bit cute. It totally freaks me out. I prefer my admirers up front.... Mom, please try to get real for once, we don't know what—or who— I'm going to have to start carrying pepper spray.... Oh, for gosh sake. Dad, talk to her, would you?"

Dad's face turned to a kind of mask as he took the phone. "Hello, Rosalie, you're welcome to join us here in Fairview if you'd like.... Yes, I take it very seriously indeed." He was using his I-am-being-calm-and-patient voice with her. "Did you see the new pictures? The pervert will be coming right in through her window next.... Yes, I said pervert. It's not right or natural. This sort of photography does not qualify as artwork, even a philistine such as myself can tell that. We need to get Kari out of that ground-floor room immediately. She's much too vulnerable there. No, I don't think I'm interfering." Dad's mask started to slip, and his voice rose slightly to override Mom's. "We'll keep you informed." He flipped the phone closed.

Before he could get his face in order, Karma said, "Dad, I'm not moving out of my room! I just got it the way I want it!"

"You're out of there, starting tonight. Riggie and I need to find a place to stay, and you're staying with us."

"No way!"

"Now, Kari, use some sense—"

"Excuse me, both of you," I put in. "May I have my cell phone back, Dad? Thank you. Can we finish eating before we start arguing?"

Dad stared at me the way he might look if something on his shoe had talked to him. Karma said, "Good idea," and got busy with her shrimp scampi. I totally lost any appetite for my rib-eye steak. It had been such a strange day that I guess I'd forgotten I never took charge.

After we left the restaurant, and after we stopped at Walgreens to get toothbrushes and a few other things, we went to Kari's sorority house. First thing, Dad checked all the door and window locks, meanwhile spreading shock and awe. All of Kari's "sisters," who by the way looked even better in person than they did in photos, squeaked like guinea pigs when they heard what was going on. Kari worked a deal with Dad. She promised him she would spend the night upstairs with three other girls. She would sleep on an inflatable bed on their floor. He agreed, grumbling, gave her a hug, and then he and I left.

We already had our room—Dad had phoned to reserve one—and the hotel was within walking distance. The Old Chahokia River Inn. Dad likes vintage hotels with ornamented Victorian ceilings and brass mailboxes between the elevators but no vending machines, game rooms, swimming pools, or anything else that I might enjoy.

Not that I cared. I was too tired to complain or even talk. I just wanted to get some sleep now that we knew Karma was safe for the time being.

Dad was tired, too, but in his case that meant he needed something to grouch at. I was available. Or maybe he'd been waiting to set me straight ever since I took charge at the restaurant. Who knows. Anyway, the minute we were alone in the hotel room, he started. "Big Rig"—enunciated with the usual sarcasm—"does your school have ROTC?"

"I wouldn't know." Worn out, I flopped on the bed.

"Joining ROTC would be a way to get to know young men your age."

"I'm not *that* lonely."

"Also, ROTC would correct your posture, and require you to get a decent haircut—"

"It's all about looks with you, isn't it?"

"Well, I hate to see my only son looking like he's made of spaghetti." He showed his teeth in a grin, pretending to be kidding, but it was never a joke, not really. "Pasta pale, skinny as a noodle—"

"Dad, not now." I wanted to sleep, and he could go on like this all night.

"Yes, now. May I remind you that you are an Ebro and your appearance reflects on me?"

I don't know why all of a sudden I snapped when I'd been through this dozens of times before, without—

Actually, I do know why I snapped. Because for once in my life, that day, Dad and I had been getting along. No, more than just getting along. We had been really together. I had felt like

Dad wanted me with him, and it had been teamwork, me and Dad scrambling to be sure Karma was safe, and I thought I'd held up my end, and we'd done good. But now instead of giving me any kind of credit, here he was criticizing me as usual.

Yeah, as usual, and that's what I'd always told myself, that it was just the way he was, just live with it—but not this time. Anger and, okay, I'll admit it, hurt feelings rocketed me off the bed. In a few steps I'd grabbed my hotel key-card and was heading out the door, yelling, "I don't have to listen to this!"

"Riggie!" Dad didn't yell; he just assumed his Gestapo voice. "Where do you think you're going?"

But I was so pissed, his tone didn't slow my momentum. "Lobby has a nice sofa." I slammed the door and headed down the hall.

Behind me I heard the door open. "Riggie!" He would never, ever in a thousand years call me Ringgold, no matter how torqued he was, any more than he would ever call Kari Karma. "Rig! Come back here this instant."

I muttered what he could do to himself not quite loud enough for him to hear, and I kept going.

"Rig!" Behind me I heard his heavy, hurrying footsteps.

Screw that. I still had my running shoes on. It took me about half a minute to get clear away from him, down a stairwell, out an exit, and across back lots in case he tried to follow me in the car. Spaghetti? Ha. Now he knew a noodle could sprint.

Walking through sleepy little Fairview, kicking the ground and totally bent out of shape, I reached for my cell phone to turn it off and realized I'd left it in the hotel room. Okay, good. When Dad tried to call me, my bed would ring. Served him right. Let him worry. I wondered whether he would call the cops to look for me. Probably not yet. I would roam around for an hour or two until I calmed down. But I wanted somebody to talk to. I wondered whether Kari was still awake.

Kari. Bunking upstairs in her sorority house.

While the pervert tried to peek in her downstairs window.

So was I really going back to the hotel?

My thoughts came together with the click of what I thought at the time was a really good idea. I stopped kicking the sidewalk and got moving.

"Change of plan," I said aloud, running.

SIX

Luckily it was such a small town I already knew my way around, and luckily I was already headed in the right direction. When I got to Walgreens, they were open, and yes! they had what I was looking for. I tried to think of anything else I might need. My hoodie was plain dark gray. Pair of gloves? Nah. I'd be okay. With the Walgreens bag in my hand, I turned toward my sister's sorority house.

Actually, I jogged, partly to get good and warm, partly because I was in a hurry, and—okay, I needed to prove, if only to myself, that spaghetti had stamina.

Years ago, when I was a skinny little kid, Dad had called me spaghetti bones. Maybe he thought it was cute, but I hadn't liked it then, either.

Once I got on campus, I ditched the plastic Walgreens bag in a trash can because it showed up too much in the night. I started cutting across the grassy areas, staying off the sidewalks and out of the lights. All of which made me feel weird, kind of guilty, like, what if somebody thought *I* was the stalker? I guess real stalkers got a thrill out of sneaking around, but I sure didn't. It made me feel like a lowlife, even though I was doing it for a good reason. It was a relief when I got to Karma's sorority house and—after checking to see there was nobody around—slipped into the shrubbery underneath the window of Kari's ground-floor bedroom, where she was not sleeping tonight.

But no way could her stalker know that.

I scrunched down behind the bushes with my knees up and my back against a chilly brick wall. With one hand I dug in the mulch and rubbed some onto my face to darken it, help me blend in. With the other hand I held my weapon.

I waited, knowing he might not show but willing to chance it.

I have no idea how long I hid in the bushes. I've always been good at going into a kind of suspended animation while I waited out one of Dad's tirades or one of Mom's art-show openings. I just zoned. Not thinking about anything in particular, but not sleeping. Watching, listening, noticing. Leaves do make a slight sound when they fall. Other things I heard depended on the changing direction of the wind. A faraway hint of music; somebody playing Bach. Girly laughter. Occasional chittery sounds: bugs, bats, birds, sleepy squirrels? Footsteps on a far sidewalk, campus cop maybe. Leaves rustling in the breeze.

Leaves rustling on the ground. Somebody walking between the trees. Slowly.

I knew it was him. I just knew, way before he reached my sister's window. Felt my heart start to pound. Flexed my hands to make sure they would work right. Tried to listen as he got closer, but now my pulse sounded so loud in my ears, all I could do was wait and watch. By now my eyes were so used to the dark that the glow from the streetlamps filtering through the trees seemed as good as daylight to me.

I could see him clearly as a silhouette approaching. Slim, even skinny, and not much taller than me. But confident, striding across the sorority house's driveway on silent shoes—they call them sneakers for a reason—then stepping between the shrubbery right up to Karma's window. Almost within my arm's reach.

Now.

I lifted my weapon—a cheap disposable camera with flash—aimed it at him, and pressed the button. The burst of intense white light staggered him as if he'd been shot and also blinded me, so I didn't see his face. And I didn't see the knife. I just stood up as I kept shooting, two ... three ... four—

With a wordless sound like a desperate animal, he lunged at me.

Which scared the breath out of me, because I hadn't expected it. For some reason I'd thought he would run away. I don't remember any knife, just a sort of freeze-frame of his face like a hockey goalie's white mask coming at me. As I tried to duck away, he grabbed my shoulder. Quickly, I shoved the camera down my pants so he couldn't get it. I tried to run, but he spun me around and punched me in the face, which was a new experience. I'd never been in a fight in my life, so I didn't mind doing what seemed sensible.

I screamed.

"Help! Help! He's killing me!" I yelled, and I kept yelling as loud as I could while I tried to fight back. I connected with some part of him, but then he nailed me and gave me a nose-bleed, knocked me onto the asphalt, banged my head hard—it's true what they say about seeing stars—and dove on top of me, trying to get the camera, I guess. I smelled him, breath in my face, sweat, body odor, rank. But not for long. He couldn't hold me down; he wasn't any bigger than I was, and spaghetti can be pretty squirmy. We rolled over and over. His fist came down sideways on my chest, hitting me—that's all it felt like. There was no pain. Nothing hurt except my hand, specifically my thumb, from trying to punch him. He hit me the same way again, and I shouted for help and clawed at his eyes, trying to make him go away. It was getting messy, blood from my nose choking me—

Then all of a sudden it was over. Lights came on, voices shouted; he got up and ran. Gone in the dark under the trees within seconds. I could see he was a pretty good sprinter. Like me again. Which made me feel weird.

I lay where I was, on the pavement, panting, checking with one hand for the camera in my pants. It was right where I'd put it.

Yes! I didn't care that I was beat up. I'd done what I'd wanted to.

The campus cop who found me a minute later didn't seem to see it that way. I told him I was fine and tried to get up, but he said, "Whoa, kid, you ain't going anywhere till we get this sorted out." He held me down, calling backup plus an ambulance through the radio on his shoulder. As girls came pouring out of the sorority house to see what the commotion was, Karma shrieked and told the cop I was her brother, but he wouldn't let her near me. I wanted to tell her stop worrying, I was fine. I think I tried to yell to her, but instead I blacked out.

The next thing I remember, people were unloading me from an ambulance at the hospital, and Kari was there, and Dad, too.

"Riggie, what *happened*?" I'd never seen that look on Dad's face before. I must have really looked like a bloody mess.

And I wanted to play it so cool, like on TV, saying, "The stalker didn't want his picture taken." But actually all I managed was, "Stalker," and I pulled the camera out of my pants and handed it to him.

"The *stalker*?" Kari squeaked. She was wearing bunny-print flannel pajamas with feet; she looked like a scared little girl.

"Stalker's picture," I mumbled. My mouth felt sick. Thick, I mean. I felt sick all over.

"I'll take custody of that," said a cop in a blue uniform, grabbing the camera from Dad. When had the cops showed up? Things were getting confusing. Cops asking me for a description of the bad guy—my size; my build; maybe even my age; young—while a crowd of people in medical scrubs and masks rolled me inside, poking a needle into my arm and shining a light into my eyes, and some guy asking me, "Did you see how long the knife was?"

"Knife?"

"You're not aware you've been stabbed?"

"No. What would he need a knife for?" But before I was done asking, I knew the answer. He had meant to force his way in through Karma's window.

That creep.

"My sister," I said. "He came to get my sister." I tried to sit up, but they pushed me down. From somewhere behind all the white-masked faces I heard my Dad's voice telling me, "Big Rig, your sister's fine."

Karma added, "I'm calling Mom!" She sounded like she was crying.

"Tell her to bring your yearbook," I said. Mom had bought a copy just for herself; and after we got home to the city after Kari's graduation, I noticed she looked at it a lot.

"What?" Kari came closer. "What did he say?"

One of the nurses answered for me. "He wants your mother to bring your yearbook." I nodded, and then I kind of checked out again.

They must have given me something for pain, because I remember bits and pieces after that, but it's all kind of fuzzy. I remember Kari saying Mom was catching a plane here, which surprised me and seemed really unnecessary if it was on my account. I remember doctors conferring and shooting dye into me and looking at me with a special machine to see how deep the stab wounds were and whether I had internal injuries. It turned out the knife was short, like a box-cutter or something, meant for forcing the window open, not for killing me. It didn't go deep or hit anything serious, but they didn't know what kind of dirt might have been on it. So they kind of power-washed the stab wounds with a nozzle thing, which didn't feel real good, then packed them with sterile gauze, bandaged them, gave me some shots—antibiotics? tetanus?—and put a splint on my nose, at which point I realized, hello, it was broken. I remember a lot of talk about whether I had a concussion or whether my brain might have bounced around inside my head and be bleeding. I thought it was stupid, but Dad and the doctors thought I ought to have a CAT scan of my head.

Meanwhile about two carloads of Kari's sorority sisters had

showed up to be there for her, which was a good thing, because Kari was getting really cold and miserable in her bunny pajamas. The girls offered to take her back to the sorority house to get some clothes. Dad said okay, as long as some of them were always with her, but she wasn't staying at the sorority house; she was moving into the hotel with her family. He passed her his hotel key-card as he ran after the people rolling me down a hallway toward radiology.

It took a while, but eventually the CAT scan showed that my precious brain was just fine, thank you very much, and I thought we were done at the hospital. I still felt fuzzy, but I woke up fast when I heard some doctor telling Dad they wanted to keep me overnight for observation. Then I remember me saying no way, I was going back to the hotel to be with Dad and Kari.

"Riggie," my father told me in his most CEO voice, "you're staying here, and that's final."

"It is not," I shot back, sitting up straight on the emergency-room bed. See, I had set a precedent, slamming out of the hotel room instead of letting Dad lecture me; that was a first. But it had felt so right to do what I had to do that I wasn't about to stop now. I told Dad, "This is what is final." My mouth hurt, and my swollen lips felt like they would pop and bleed; but I ignored them and kept talking. "You can either take me with you and know where I am, or you can leave me here and not know where I am, because I promise you within five minutes I will be out of this place."

"You will do no such thing. You scared me silly running off that way."

Something in his voice sugared my heart, like he wasn't just being top dog, he really did care. Even though he was command-ing, "Don't you ever pull a stunt like that on me again."

"I hope I never have to." And I hoped he could tell through my thick voice that I wasn't just talking back. I totally meant it. "But I *will* walk out of this hospital if you try to make me stay here." I couldn't let him sideline me and forget about me. I needed to see Kari's high school yearbook.

"Riggie, what are you trying to prove? Look what you've accomplished so far. Here I am worrying about you *and* Kari instead of being with Kari."

That hit my gut, because he was right. I had been kind of stupid getting hurt, even though I also got the photos. I admitted to myself that yeah, I was trying to prove something. To him.

But all I said was, "So stop worrying about me. I'm fine, and I'm coming with you."

"Riggie," my father told me in his most storm-trooper voice, "You will stay here." Dad tried to stare me down.

"I will not." I stared back. I wasn't angry, just determined.

Dad seemed like he was trying to be angry but couldn't get the blast furnace going. He blinked, shook his head, peered at me again. "Riggie..."

I pushed off the bed and stood up. "Karma's stalker could have run away, or he could have just fought to get the camera; but no-o-o-o, he knifed me," I said. I sounded grimmer and angrier than Dad did. "He's a mean bastard and we're wasting time. Let's go."

Arguing only a little along the way, we did.

SEVEN

First thing when we got back to the hotel, Dad asked at the desk whether Kari had signed in; and yes, she had. Next thing I sat down at the computer in the lobby, pulled up KarmaEbro.net, and scrolled to the bottom.

The red roses were gone.

Instead there were some pictures I did not study closely. No guy wants to see his sister through the crack in the curtains, undressing. There was a big close-up of a road-killed rattlesnake with its guts oozing, and there were sulfur-yellow words on the black background.

BETRAYED
BETRAYED
BETRAYED
BETRAYED

**BITCH EVERY DAY YOU SEE ME AND ACT LIKE
YOU DON'T KNOW I EXIST LIKE YOU THINK YOUR
SOME SORT OF GODDAMN GODDESS BITCH YOU
WILL PAY I WOULD LIKE TO RIP THAT SMILE OFF
YOUR FACE RIP YOUR LIPS OFF AND PUT THEM IN
THE BLENDER PROUD SNOT HOW SUPERIOR WILL
YOU FEEL WHEN I TAKE YOU**

It went on but I couldn't read any more. It was as if he had vomited the yellow words onto the black computer screen. They nauseated me.

Looking over my shoulder, Dad said in a strained voice, "I'll call the cops." He headed toward the windows to use his cell phone.

I swallowed a couple of times, then managed to call after him, "Tell them he was stalking her in Sumac, too, so if they can find somebody who moved here from back east—"

Dad spun around. "He was already stalking her in *Sumac?* What makes you think that?" he demanded, standing with his cell phone poised, staring at me as if he'd never seen me before.

"The photos. Some of the backgrounds look familiar to me. Gotta be Sumac. And Kari's bangs. She had bangs till she went to college. It's hard to tell without a magnifying glass, depending on the angle, but I think I see bangs on some of the long-distance shots."

Dad had gotten the dazed, uncomprehending look my explanations usually gave him as he pulled out the card Officer Steverson had given him at the hospital and thumbed the number. We had our very own detective now. He said he'd be at the hotel in five minutes.

I wobbled over to the sofa, and it wasn't till then that I realized the hotel night staff was gawking at me and whispering as they set up for the "complimentary continental breakfast." Okay, bandages on my head and shoulder, splint on my nose, hospital gown instead of a shirt, blood on my jeans. I guess I looked like Halloween a couple weeks early.

"Riggie," Dad asked all of a sudden, "can I get you coffee? You look like you need something."

I never drank coffee before, but I said, "With lots of sugar. And a straw."

He put in lots of cream, too. And he was right, I needed something. Processing that hot stuff through my sore mouth didn't taste good, but it felt terrific.

It was getting a little bit light outside when the balding, rumpled cop I remembered from the hospital came in through the revolving door. Detective Steverson did a slight double take when he saw me, then came over and handed me a brown envelope. "Your photos, son." Dad led him to the computer and showed him the latest crud. He took it in, nodded kind of wearily, and looked at my father. "As we told you from the first, Mr. Ebro, we can't arrest a person just for putting nonpornographic photographs on the Internet. And we don't have any proof that it's the same person who assaulted your son."

"But you are going to arrest him for attacking Riggie."

"Of course."

"Good. Proof that he was stalking my daughter can come later," said Dad quietly. "We got anything to go on?"

"Your son's photos."

Which I was studying. Four of them. The first one, showing

Kari's stalker in profile at her window ready to break in, was the best. In the other three, showing him coming at me, the flash had kind of flattened his features and the expression on his face stretched them. He barely looked human.

"I'm making copies for all the patrolmen plus the campus force," the detective said. "First thing tomorrow—heck, today. It's morning. Within a couple of hours, we'll have all the officers we can assign going door to door, starting with the apartments near campus."

"I don't think he'll be living in an apartment," I put in.

Steverson and my father turned to me, startled, like I was a talking dog.

I said, "I smelled him. He absolutely, totally reeks of wood smoke. Nobody heats an apartment with a woodstove."

The detective asked, "Could it have been cigarette smoke?"

"No. I've been around wood smoke for years at summer camps. It's different than cigarette smoke. And when you heat with wood, it really saturates your clothes, your hair, everything. Plus, this guy had B.O., like he never takes a shower. Which is maybe part of an antisocial attitude, and for sure he can't hold a job that way. So he's probably getting by in some trailer or cabin way back in the hills where he can pick up his firewood for free."

The detective looked doubtful but asked, "Anything else you noticed, Riggie?"

"Just that he's truly scary, the way he jumped me. You don't know what he's going to do, you know? He followed my sister here all the way from the East Coast."

Dad said in a kind of choked voice, "Are you sure he did that? Could he really be that obsessed?"

"When Mom gets here with the yearbook, we'll see."

The detective said, "Perhaps Karma would recognize him from the photos Riggie took."

"I'll get her down here," Dad said. He went to the house phone and called our room.

He let it ring for a long time. "She's not answering," he said finally, slamming the phone down. "She must be sound asleep. Rig—" But I already had my key-card out for him. Rather than waiting for an elevator, he ran up the stairs two at a time. I saw a reaction on the cop's face that I couldn't take. It made me turn away. I didn't want to think yet. Time seemed to slow down, and nothing made any sense. Not even Dad's face, pale as pasta, when he came panting downstairs.

Or what he said. "She's not there."

Like a toad-brain, I croaked, "What?"

"She's not *there*. Where is she?"

Dad ran to the registration desk, and I saw the people there going wide-eyed as they talked with him, and pointing to the elevator. Meanwhile I whipped out my cell phone and called Kari, but all I got was her voice mail. I closed the phone. Dad was walking toward me. We didn't have to say anything. We just looked at each other.

Detective Steverson stopped Dad and asked, "Is her car in the parking lot?"

"Probably not, because her sorority sisters brought her here. I'm told they waved and watched her step into the elevator."

"You're saying something happened to her between this lobby and your *room*? Which elevator did she take?"

While they headed back toward the front desk to ask, I got up, stumbled to the concierge's desk, and asked for a phone book. But how the heck do you look up Greek letters? The woman behind the desk saw me fumbling. "What do you need? Perhaps I can find it."

Actually she had the number on a list taped to her desk. She dialed Kari's sorority house on her phone and handed it to me.

It rang a long time before some girl answered, sounding really sleepy. The way I asked, "Does anybody know where Kari is?" seemed to wake her up in a hurry.

"She's not at the hotel?"

"Not in the room, no, and she's not answering her phone."

"Is this her brother?"

I felt like telling her no, it was pizza delivery, but I just said yes.

"I'll check to see if anybody knows anything." Then in the background I could hear her calling, "Has anybody seen Kari? I mean since we left her at the hotel?" After some yelling back and forth with the other girls, she came back to the phone and said, "Nobody has any idea where she could be," and she sounded almost as scared as I felt.

"Riggie, tell them to notify campus security," Dad called to me from across the lobby. I did that, then hung up and just leaned on the concierge's desk because I felt too weak to get back to the sofa. I watched a bunch of cops in uniform hurry in and spread out to search the hotel, like, maybe they'd find bloodstains? I felt really sick.

After a moment I tuned in that Dad was talking to me. "...Big Rig, try not to worry so much. Think. I don't believe that creep had time to go home, put that poison on the computer, and then get back here—"

I mumbled, "Not home. Some Internet café. We were in that emergency room practically all night, and it's my fault."

Dad seemed to agree, because he didn't say anything. But maybe that's because he was watching Detective Steverson walk toward us with an armload of stuff.

Gym bag. Football jacket. Cell phone. And a watch with the wristband broken.

"It looks like she put up a fight," he said, his voice quiet and careful. "The patrolmen found these scattered up and down the stairwell to the parking lot."

"Are you sure they're my daughter's?" Dad was not as successful in being quiet.

"Her wallet and ID are in the gym bag."

"That's Kari's cell. And her watch." I hadn't meant to say it aloud, but the words kind of bled out of me.

Dad looked at me, then grabbed me by the arm. "Riggie, for God's sake, sit down before you fall down." He steered me toward the sofa.

I grabbed the armrest to ease myself down, and then, just when it seemed like I could not possibly handle anything more, a shocked voice squeaked, "Ringgold!"

Mom.

Right there in the hotel lobby was my mother, ditching her flower-print suitcase and hurrying to me, her eyes wide blue exclamations. "Riggie, how—what—I simply could not believe it, and I still can't—"

I folded onto the sofa, and Mom bent over me, patting whatever parts of my hair and face she could reach through the bandages. "Why would anyone hurt you, sweetie? Your poor nose! You poor thing!"

Damn, she got to me. I wanted to lay my head on her shoulder and bawl like a baby. I was hurt, my sister was snatched by a pervert, I felt like it was my fault because maybe he wouldn't have done it so soon if I hadn't spooked him. I just wanted to cry. But this was no time to feel sorry for myself.

"Mom, sit down." I had to make my voice hard to keep it under control. "Listen. Kari's missing."

She sat down like I said, but she seemed not to hear me at all. "What sort of person *did* this to you, Riggie?"

"Never mind me!" I wanted to scream, *The weirdo has Kari! The stalker has her!* "Did you bring Kari's yearbook with you?"

"Yes, although I have no idea—"

"Where *is* it?"

"In my suitcase. Ringgold, hadn't you better—"

"Get it!"

"—take some Tylenol and go to bed?"

"Mom," I said in a pretty good imitation of Dad, "get the yearbook. Now."

Looking bewildered, which wasn't unusual for her, she stood up and went for her suitcase. In the scarlet getup she was wearing that day, she looked kind of like Little Red Riding Hood going to visit Grandma. But I wasn't the wolf. The big bad wolf was out there in the dusk of dawn somewhere.

As I grabbed the yearbook, I heard Dad say, "Rosalie?" He'd just noticed she was there. "Rosalie." His voice was numb. "Rig, did you tell her?"

"Tried to. She's not hearing me." Paging through the yearbook like mad, I didn't look up. "Dad, if you show her the new stuff on the computer, maybe she'll get a clue."

For a couple of precious minutes, everybody left me alone, and I took the time to make myself think. To check my reasoning.

Creep had been stalking Kari in Sumac. In some of the long-distance shots, aside from Kari's bangs, sometimes I recognized a familiar background. Had to be Sumac.

The stalker was a kid around Kari's age. I knew that from the encounter at the sorority-house window. If he was from Sumac, he should have been in Sumac High School.

But probably not in Kari's class. She knew everybody in her class. I mean literally everybody—she made that a priority of her job as class president—so she would have noticed if he'd been in her class in high school and then she had glimpsed him here in Fairview. Either he was awfully good at staying out of sight or, more likely, he was an underclassman.

And a misfit. Not stupid but not happy and definitely not an achiever. Nothing better to do than follow my sister around.

I found the pages of class pictures. Freshman, sophomore, junior, senior. I checked through the senior section quickly just in case. Those photos were big enough, it was easy to see he wasn't there.

Working backward, I started on the Junior section. Now the photos were smaller and you couldn't tell much from them, but I watched for ones with space underneath. Like, there had been no space under Kari's photo; it was crowded with Chorus 1234, Orchestra 1234, Student Council 234, National Merit Semifinalist, stuff like that. But a loner's photo would have a completely blank space, or maybe it would have nothing except computer club. Something like that.

Mom and Dad came back. Without paying attention, I heard them arguing over my head. "There has to be a simple, harmless explanation," Mom was saying. "I refuse to believe she's in real danger."

"Believe whatever you have to, Rosalie." Dad sounded tired. "But if you look at what he did to Riggie, there's reason to be concerned."

"What makes you think he has her? She might have just gone to McDonald's."

"You can't really believe that."

"What I mean is, something came up—"

"The stalker came up. Last night he tried to make entry through her window, but Riggie caught him," Dad said. "You saw his reaction on the Web site. He has her, all right."

"But why would he want to kidnap Kari? We're well-to-do, but we're not *rich*."

Dad didn't say anything. Mom was talking as if somebody had snatched Kari for ransom, and when Mom gets like that, Cleopatra, Queen of Denial, it kind of stuns the speech out of you.

Mom went on. "Who is this person? What does he want? What do we know about him?"

Before Dad could answer, I said, "We know his name."

EIGHT

"You found him?" Dad exclaimed so loudly that Detective Steverson came hurrying over.

"I think so." I pointed at a small photo of a boy who had been a junior when Kari was a senior. A photo without any activities printed under it. A photo without a smile. A photo with lonesome eyes staring. The same eyes I had seen staring, spookier under darker circumstances.

The detective looked from that photo to the ones I'd taken and said, "I'll be damned." Scribbling on his notepad, he added, "Gotta call downtown right away, have them run his name through the computer."

His name was Curt Crocker. No middle name or initial.

Waiting to hear back about him would have been unbearable—for me, anyway—if it weren't that the hotel staff had caught on to the situation and swarmed us with food and sympathy. They loaded plates, filled cups and glasses, carried breakfast into the lobby for us, sat us down, and coaxed us to eat as if we were children. Still on the sofa, I found myself swallowing scrambled eggs and sipping orange juice while a lady in a white uniform stood over me yelling for somebody to bring me applesauce, I needed soft food. Dad drank coffee and nibbled a bagel. The detective had a doughnut. Yeah, really, stereotype and all. Mom sat as far as possible from Dad, drank hot chocolate, and ate every kind of Danish they gave her, telling them what nice, good people they were, how kind, how very kind.

Dad said to no one in particular, "She has always depended on the kindness of strangers."

Feeling better because of applesauce and kindness somehow only made me feel worse about Kari. The contrast, these good people versus that pervert.

Kari. God, please let her be okay.

Curt Crocker. A name. Would it help?

Some uniformed cops came in to talk with Detective Steverson. Dad stood up and went over to them. I set aside my plate, still half full of food, struggled up—ouch! Once I moved, every part of me hurt—but I limped over.

"...only address is a Fairview post-office box," one of the cops was saying. "He had a juvenile rap sheet back East. Vandalism, shoplifting, arson."

"DMV says he drives a 1982 Chevy S-10 pickup," said the other cop. "Figure it's a junker."

Glancing at me, the detective said, "You were right, son. He followed her here to Fairview."

"We don't know where he lives?" Dad asked urgently.

"Not yet." Detective Steverson nodded at the uniformed

officers, and they headed for the door. "They're doing everything they can, and people at the station are working the phones, trying to get a lead on this Curt Crocker. Wait a minute"—as his phone vibrated. He answered it, "Yeah."

A pause.

"Yeah? Good work. Okay, I'll be right there." He jammed the phone back into its case on his belt and turned to my father, who looked ready to break or explode—same thing, in a way. "They found Karma's Jetta where she left it in the hospital parking lot, but it's been vandalized. Windows smashed, graffiti all over it, threats against your daughter similar to those on the computer. Try to think positively, Mr. Ebro. With the evidence we hold now, we have probable cause to call in the FBI, although it will take them a few hours to get here. Meanwhile we'll question everybody around the hospital as well as here at the hotel. Maybe we'll be able to pick up a trail." He headed for the door, with my dad right at his side.

I tried to follow but couldn't keep up. Dad saw me through the revolving door, came back around, and told me, "Riggie, for God's sake, get some rest before you land back in the hospital." He sounded intense but not mean. He looked at my mother. "Rosalie, take care of him, would you? He has the room keycard. Put him to bed." Without waiting for a reply, he swung around the door again and hustled after the detective. I watched them get into an unmarked car and pull away.

I barely heard Mom talking to me. "Ringgold, I'm sure your father and the police will take care of everything."

"Uh."

"Your father is a very competent man."

"Um."

"And he's absolutely right that you do belong in bed. What room are you in?"

I didn't answer. Just stood staring.

She gave a big patience-on-a-monument sigh, went to the desk, talked to a clerk. She came back with an extra key-card. "Riggie, come on." When I didn't respond, she took me by the elbow on my less-bandaged side and steered me toward the elevator. Like a puppet, I dragged along with her.

It wasn't until we got into the room and I actually sat on the bed that I came back to life, realizing how ridiculous this was. No way could I sleep. How could I possibly spend the day lying there staring at the ceiling?

I stood up. "Mom, we can't do this."

She pushed me back down. "Let me help you get your shoes off."

"Let my shoes alone. Listen," I demanded, eye to eye with her as she sat on Dad's bed, "do you *understand* what's happening to Kari?"

"I'm sure your father will find her soon."

"But this Curt Crocker guy has her now—"

"We don't know that."

"Mom, look at me! Don't you see what he wants to do to her?"

She took "look at me" kind of literally. "You think he might break her nose?"

"Mom. Get a clue. He stabbed me. If the knife had been long enough he would have killed me. He could kill her." I had to take a breath, because Mom's face—God, I felt like the meanest, lowest thing on two feet, as cruel as the stalker, but I had to do it.

I said, "Mom, he spells it out right there on the Internet. He thinks he owns her. He's taken her, and he's going to want her to do whatever he says, and if she won't, he's going to beat her—"

"But *why?*" Mom cried out in real pain. "He—the roses and everything, he adores her!"

"Not after what he did to her car. Now it's *adored*. Past tense." The word *adored* was way too good for him, but I let it go, because Mom was actually listening. I forced my swollen mouth to go on speaking, softer. "He thought he was courting her and she was rejecting him, but it's all in his mind. He's sick, Mom. Look at the pictures he took. He kept getting nastier, like, more graphic, then last night he came with a knife to break into her bedroom." It wasn't my fault, I realized. He had planned to abduct my sister before he knew anything about me. "He's mean, Mom, and I think he's crazy. He really believes Kari belongs to him and he has the right to—to do things to her." My own words shot me to my feet. "Mom, we have to go find her."

It was too much for Mom to handle. Hugging herself like she was cold, looking up at me, she blurted, "Now, Riggie, that's nonsense. How would *we* find her?"

Actually, I had no idea, but I knew how to push Mom's buttons. "You saying we don't have as good a chance as anybody else?"

"Why, of course we do!" She sat up straighter. "But your father said—"

"Since when do you do whatever Dad says?"

Mom almost smiled.

I pressed on. "You have a rental car?"

"Courtesy car, actually, from the local airport, free of charge.

They were so, so nice, arranging an Angel Flight to bring me here directly."

"Good."

"It's not good that you were hurt and in the emergency room!"

"I mean good, you have a car." I grabbed my cell phone and stuffed it into the pocket of my jeans. "Wonderful." This time I was the one towing Mom by the elbow, toward the door. "You have the keys? Let's go."

"Go where?"

"I don't know. But anything's better than doing nothing, right?"

"I suppose so," she said doubtfully as I got her into the elevator.

But in the lobby she balked. "Riggie, wait. Where's your jacket? You can't go outside like that." I looked down and saw I was still wearing the faded flowery cotton thing the hospital had put on me. "You'll freeze."

Oh, no. If we lost momentum now, I might never get Mom moving again. "Is it really cold outside?" I appealed to the people at the desk, who felt like old friends by now.

"Yes, it is. It's frigid," said one of the women; and then they all started talking about how unusually cold it was, although thank goodness there was no wind; how frosty for October, even though the sun was shining in a clear blue sky; and the aspens were absolutely gorgeous on the hillsides. While I stood there, feeling my brain strain for—something—

Oh. Oh, my gosh.

The manager trotted out of the gift shop with a big navy blue zip-up fleece jacket. She clopped over to me in her high heels and wrapped it around my shoulders. "There you go."

"Thank you," I told her, and I'd never meant it more. "Thank you so much. Mom, come on."

But already inertia had taken hold of her. "Riggie, I don't know. What can we do?"

"I know exactly what we can do, and we're the only ones likely to do it! Come on!"

She heard the sudden hope in my voice and moved. Through the revolving door, outside, and yeah, it was cold. Thank you, God, for making it be cold with no wind.

"Car," I told Mom.

"Riggie, what—"

"Car! Where?"

It was in the hotel parking lot, and I wouldn't say another word until we were both seat-belted in and she had the heater going. My mind was busy with too many questions. Where could I get a map? Which was the most likely direction? If I called Detective Steverson, would he listen? Or would he get me in trouble with Dad?

One question got answered the minute I looked at the car dash. "Mom! You've got a GPS!"

"What? I never use those things."

I turned it on and zoomed it out until we had a complete map of Fairview. The Chahokia River pretty much took care of the whole east side from north to south. There was only one bridge. Maybe Curt Crocker lived across the bridge in East Fairview, but my gut told me no way. He wouldn't put that big river between him and Kari.

"Just drive till we get to the edge of town," I told Mom.

"Which way?"

"Any way! Go!"

She put the car in gear and headed out of the hotel parking lot and down Main Street. In an accusing tone she said, "I thought you knew what we were looking for."

"I do," I said, teeth clenched because I was turning to look through the side and back windows, ducking my head to glimpse the horizon, trying to spot the hillsides covered with forests in blazing fall foliage, and every movement hurt like hell.

"Well, what is it?" Mom demanded.

"Smoke! The smoke from his woodstove."

NINE

One super thing about Mom, she never tells anybody they're crazy. Dad or the detective would have blown me off like a bug right away, but Mom is such a space cadet or maybe a genius that she'll believe anything is possible, even if she doesn't understand it.

She asked, "Smoke signals?"

"Sort of. I know the guy heats with wood because I smelled it on him. Nobody reeks of smoke that way unless they live with it day and night, not just to toast marshmallows. This guy, figure he took Kari to his place. I think he lives out in the woods because, um—" He stank, and I just knew he was a loner, but how could I explain that to Mom?

"Because that's where the firewood is," Mom prompted.

"Yes!" Pure Mom, simple and totally true. "So we're looking for woods with chimney smoke going up."

Mom nodded, remarking, "You know, you hardly ever see

a chimney actually smoking anymore, since everybody's heating with electricity or natural gas."

I glanced at the buildings in town. She was right. No smoke. Great, but I wanted to see woods, not buildings.

I told Mom, "We've got to find a high place where there's a view."

"Or if we get on the bridge and drive to the other side of the river, then look back, we ought to see a nice panorama of the entire area."

Trust an artist to know how to see a panorama. "Mom, you're the best. Let's go."

It took only a few minutes to find the bridge; I navigated her there with the GPS. Remarking that she felt sure Kari was fine, Mom pressed the gas pedal to the floor and zoomed across the mile-long bridge, at the far end of which she swerved into a scenic overlook and stopped the car without bothering to park properly. We had the place to ourselves, anyway.

Mom popped out and stood studying her panorama. It took me a minute longer to get my stiff, sore bod out of the car.

"Good light," Mom said, whatever that meant. Maybe that the sun was behind our backs and not up high enough yet to flatten things like my camera flash; Fairview looked very 3-D. We could see the folds of the hills.

Lots of hills, almost mountains. Covered with yellow-orange-tan fall trees.

Too many hillsides, too much woods. I felt hopeless. "There's smoke," I said, but my voice sounded hollow even to me, because the smoke was blobby and dark, like somebody was burning tires.

"That looks like it's coming from the railroad yards next to the river." Mom put one hand like a visor over her eyes and slowly scanned the hills from left to right as if she were reading a book. "There," she said suddenly, with satisfaction yet totally matter-of-fact, as if she had expected nothing less.

"Where?" I couldn't see anything.

"Third church steeple," Mom told me, "then look up and a little bit to the left. White smoke. Do you see it?"

And yes, I did see it, like a chalk line drawn on the rust-colored trees and the blue sky.

A chalk line leading to one hill among many.

Was it really pointing to Kari? It wasn't the only wood smoke in the world. Now that I had spotted it, I could see three or four others, farther off. But this one looked like it was behind Kari's sorority house.

A kind of Bohemian goulash of pain churned up my insides. Kari was dead, I knew most likely she was dead, but I couldn't go there; I just had to find her. If not dead she was hurt, slashed, mutilated, and not only that, but...

But I had to push it all away so I could keep going. Find her. Being with Mom, who naturally declared nothing bad could possibly have happened, helped me pretend I didn't think things were so bad, either. And—I know this is backward—being hurt myself helped me stay strong. After things got better I could go ahead and feel miserable.

Eyes on the white wisp of smoke, I told Mom, "Come on, let's go. There has to be a way to get there."

But we didn't know it. We didn't know our way around those hills at all.

Some help would have been nice. Even though I had practically no hope the cops would give it—they were still pounding on apartment doors around campus—I knew I had to try.

I didn't have Detective Steverson's number. Dad had it, but no way was I going to call Dad, because he had ordered me to stay in the hotel. So, as Mom drove back across the bridge to Fairview, I called 911 and asked them to please patch me through to Detective Steverson.

"But what is the nature of your emergency?"

"The nature of my emergency is that I need to talk with Detective Steverson!"

"Fire, police, ambulance?"

Helicopter, I thought, but all I said was, "Detective Steverson!"

The detective recognized my voice right away when they finally put me through, and he did not sound thrilled. "Riggie? What's the problem?"

"You need to put somebody up in a helicopter." I tried to talk clearly because there was a lot of background noise on his end, people yakking, car engines. "You have a police helicopter?"

"Yes, but what—"

"Look for smoke," I explained, "from a woodstove, smoke coming up from the trees. It's a cold day. The creep took Kari to his shack and made a fire. I—"

"Son, I can't justify hundreds of dollars to have the helicopter chase smoke! There must be dozens—"

"Maybe, but there's one in particular coming from a hill directly behind Kari's sorority—"

"It still could come from anybody's fire."

"Detective Steverson," I begged, "listen to me. Please. It's a thin white line of smoke, and I need help to find it!"

"Son, you need to get some sleep and let me do my job."

I bit my lip to make myself ask, "Is my dad there?" Maybe Dad could convince him.

"No."

"He isn't? But he went with you—"

"To the station. *Good-bye*, Riggie." He hung up.

And that was that. Like I'd told Mom, I knew what to do, but we were the only ones who would do it.

Meanwhile, Mom was driving through Fairview, zigzagging along back streets and, out of habit, admiring the scenery. She commented, "Oh, look. Isn't that different?" as we passed the cemetery with the Indian mound where Kari liked to go study.

"No time, Mom."

"I know, I know! I'm sorry, I can't help—Do I have us headed in the right direction?"

"Yes. Yeah, you're doing good." We were behind campus; the cemetery told me that. I studied the GPS to navigate us toward country, wooded hillsides, a white feather of smoke. "Mom, hang a left. Okay, we're on West Hummel, which turns into Old Buckshot Road." Almost as soon as I said it, we began to see fields and trees beyond the edge of town, and a minute later we drove through pastures sloping up to wooded hillsides half bare but still bright with pointy aspens like candle flames.

Screw yellow and orange. Scanning all over the place, I wanted white. White smoke.

"There it is," Mom said placidly, pointing.

I don't know how she saw it, floating up like a ghost ribbon from between the folds of the hills. "Take the next right!"

With a glance at the GPS, she said, "I don't see any." Not until we got to Buckshot, seven miles ahead.

"Take this dirt road!"

"If it was a road, wouldn't it be on the GPS?"

"Just turn!"

She did. The one-lane, rutted gravel excuse for a road bumped us across the farmland and up into the woods. Looking all around, I couldn't see a thing except shadows, brush, and trees. No white feather of smoke. The road got narrower and narrower until it just stopped.

God, was this whole day doomed to be a dead end? Once we got into the forest, we couldn't see where we were going, and Kari—what might be happening to Kari?

Or might already have happened?

Don't. Don't go there.

Mom put the car in reverse and, not too placid anymore, backed down the road really fast, putting us in the ditch once or twice, until she found a place where we could turn around.

Back on the paved road, she stepped on the gas. She wasn't saying anything about Kari, but I think, like me, she had started to sweat.

"Phew, Riggie, you're ripe," she muttered. I guess my deodorant had worn off a while back, plus I was still wearing yesterday's blood-splattered jeans.

"It's not me. It's the pigs," I said as we zoomed past a pig farm by another dirt road, where we turned right again. This one also took us up into the woods, but then it looped around for what seemed forever—well, we could only go about ten miles an hour, bouncing and swaying along the muddy ruts—and then it dumped us back out almost exactly where we had started.

"Is that the same damn pig farm?" Mom asked.

Mom hardly ever said *damn*. Me, I could have screamed, and not only from frustration. Every inch of my beat-up bod ached from riding on these rough roads. And I felt sick to my stomach from the things I was trying not to think.

We kept going. The next dirt road took us up into the hills yet again, past a few hunting shacks, and instead of getting narrower, it branched like a Y. Mom asked, "Which way?"

"Umm..." As the GPS was no help, I looked at the compass. "Right." I figured we'd come far enough west that now we needed to go north.

But the dirt track doubled back and took us east, then south. We hadn't yet met a single car, but people did live back here. We saw two or three pretty nice cabins.

"We need to get farther up, to the north," Mom said.

"I *know*." Finally another road of sorts, maybe a logging trail, headed off to the left. I said, "Turn there."

She did, and when she came to a place where the trees thinned out, she stopped the car, got out, and scanned the sky all around. When she got back in the car, I could tell from her face that she hadn't seen any smoke.

"It's a no-win," she said. "We see where we need to go, but when we get there, we can't see where we're going."

She was starting to sound kind of far away. I said as tough as I could, "Look, it's better than sitting in the hotel doing nothing, isn't it?"

"I guess." She put the car in gear, and we bumped onward.

The road was nothing but two dirt tire marks with grass in between. Downhill, uphill. Another dirt-track crossing. We took it because it looked a little more traveled, with less grass, more mud. Mom turned left again because that way seemed to go kind of north. We still hadn't seen anybody besides us up here.

We joggled along in tense silence. Even during the divorce I'd never got such tense vibes from Mom, she was so all about positive energy.

"One of these roads has to take us *somewhere*," I blurted out.

The car hiccuped a couple of times, and then the engine died.

Mom tried to start it. And tried, and tried again, cranking until I said, "You're wearing out the battery."

"*Damn*," Mom said, about as unpeaceful as I've ever heard her. "I haven't scraped the undercarriage, I'd swear to that. What's the matter with the stupid thing?"

Simple enough, but I couldn't bear to say it.

"Oh, damn it to hell and back again," she cried. "We're out of gas!"

Yes, and I hated myself because I hadn't thought to remind her to fill it up.

But being Mom, next moment she brightened. "Oh, well. We'll call Triple-A."

Oh, right. Like that was really going to help Kari.

But there was nothing else to do.

Anyhow, when things were getting bad, Mom always went on automatic pilot. She rummaged in her purse, got out her AAA card, and deployed her cell phone.

I was amazed she actually got a signal, back in these hills.

But, "That's stupid," she said, frowning, after she dialed. "They say I am in violation of my calling regulations."

I groaned. Mom's phone was so—so Jurassic. I started to pull out my cell.

Mom said, "I read someplace that any cell phone anywhere can call 911."

"Mom, don't—"

But she already had. And yes, it had worked. She was chirping to the dispatcher, "We're out of gas. Miles from anyplace."

Then she looked at me blankly. "They want to know where we are, exactly."

"Good luck."

"Um, we're northwest of Fairview, in the woods, but none of these dirt roads—jeep trails, is that what you call them? They don't seem to have names."

Peering at the GPS, I told her the latitude and longitude in degrees divided into minutes and seconds. Latitude 40-some and longitude 110-some. She repeated the numbers to 911.

Then she listened briefly, her smile slipping a little bit. "I see...yes, I understand it will take a while.... We appreciate your help. Thank you."

She turned off her cell phone, dropped it back into her purse, and sat with a peculiar look on her face.

"They are notifying the police," she told me. "To come rescue us."

TEN

I put my head in my hands and groaned. This was worse than embarrassing. This was catastrophic. The police needed to be looking for Kari, not for us. *We* needed to be looking for Kari, and here we sat.

But Mom, being Mom, said, "Oh, well," and got out of the car. Knowing her, I understood she was hoping to find something painterly and wonderful, like maybe a purple mushroom on a rotten log, to save these particular moments of the day.

She wandered up the so-called road. I had to watch her so she wouldn't get lost like a little kid.

She crouched by the ditch at the side of the road to study water or pebbles or something. She got up and moved on to some dried weeds with prickly brown heads. An artist browsing for whatever, she meandered a bit farther down the road—

Then like lightning had struck she lifted her head and, whoa, she stopped looking like my mother! Ditched her smile. Seemed to get taller. Like a redcoat soldier. Make that a redcoat general, without the white wig. The way she beckoned for me, I didn't just heave myself out of the car and limp to her. I ran.

"Do you smell it?" she whispered when I stood beside her.

Panting, I couldn't figure it out at first. Then it hit me.

Strong.

Wood smoke.

We would never have smelled it in the car with the heater going. We would never have found the place if the car hadn't run out of gas where it did. We would have driven right past it.

But now without a word we literally followed our noses. Along the muddy road, around a curve. Mom stuck a finger in her mouth and held it up to feel where exactly the wind was coming from. I did the same. The side of your finger the air is moving toward feels cold.

We looked at each other and both nodded toward a steep bank going down from the side of the road. Mom went over and stepped off what looked like the edge of a cliff, like she would land in a thicket of hemlock trees. But as I followed her, my feet found mud with a little gravel mixed in. A barely there track angled off the road's bend and plunged down the hillside past the hemlocks.

We followed it as softly as we could, not speaking, stopping every few steps to listen. We heard nothing, but now we could see the smoke, a faint fog of white, as well as smell it.

A few steps more and we began to catch glimpses of metallic white through the hemlocks. At the very bottom of the ravine, deep in shadow, rusted a trailer.

I caught Mom by the arm to stop her when I saw what was parked in the mud by the trailer: a small, boxy truck so old and dirty it was hard to tell, but it could have been blue.

"Mom," I whispered, "is that a 1982 Chevy?"

"I don't know," she whispered back. "Maybe."

For a moment we both stared in silence, and then I whispered, "What do you think?" and Mom knew right away I was not talking about the undersized truck. I was talking about Curt Crocker. Was this really where he lived?

"Only one way to find out," Mom said, and she started striding down the dirt track.

I ran after her and grabbed her by the arm. "Mom, what are you doing?"

She turned to look at me as if I had two heads. "Ringgold, it's a no-brainer," she declared. "If Kari is in there, I need to be with her. And if she isn't in there, we need to find out where she is." As Mom started off again, she added, "You stay here; call the cavalry."

I'd never seen her so decisive, not even when she left Dad. She stunned me. I stood there with my teeth airing.

She turned a hairpin corner around the hemlocks, out of sight.

God, Riggie, get moving! I dove into the hemlocks, on my belly to make no noise, scooting along a thick layer of needles below the hanging branches, until I got to the other side of the thicket, and—yes, right where I needed to be. I stared at the trailer door—an inner door and a storm door with three wooden steps—from maybe twenty feet away.

There I lay, hidden under the bushes. Stalking a stalker.

I glanced up. Smoke rose like a white feather above the stovepipe.

I hoped it was the right place. I dreaded it was the right place. I hurt. Mostly inside.

Mom marched up the three wooden steps to a plywood plat-form, opened the storm door, tried the knob of the inside door, then knocked. And knocked, and just kept knocking like she would never go away.

Seemed like hours, the way my heart was beating me up. Probably was a minute. Then the door opened a little bit, and the guy inside started to slip out as if he meant to talk to his visitor on the porch.

I saw his face.

It was him.

Creep.

Window-peeping pervert.

Stabbed me. Grabbed Kari.

One glimpse, and I forgot all about having a broken nose or stab wounds or any kind of pain to slow me down. I didn't feel anything but energy, adrenaline, ready to charge. But Mom was ahead of me, her Converse sneaker in the door as he tried to close it. No taller than he was but a lot heavier, she took him by surprise and blew right through him. She barged on in, pushing him ahead of her. A moment later I heard her cry, "Kari! Oh, Kari, what *happened* to you?"

I did not hear my sister reply.

But I knew Mom was talking *to* her. Kari was there.

I dashed out of the hemlocks and sprinted, slipping in the mud, to the steps at the trailer door, where I might have been stupid enough to keep going if I hadn't heard a squeaky adolescent male voice yell, "You come any closer, I'll kill her!"

He sounded panicky but quite sincere. I stopped. My heart stopped for a minute. The world seemed to stop.

Survivor instinct kicked in—my sister's survival, not mine. I crouched so I wouldn't be seen through the half-open door as I pulled out my cell phone to call 911.

But there was no signal.

I tried anyway. Nine. One. One.

Silence.

Silence on my cell phone. But inside the trailer Curt Crocker babbled, "I ought to kill her anyway. I need to kill her. I—"

"Why would you want to do that?" My mother sounded just as sincere as he did, but pleasant and a little bewildered. "You gave her those beautiful roses. I thought you loved her."

"I do love her! Years now I've practically worshiped her. But she..."

Keep him talking, Mom, I thought, easing to my feet. Bent over to stay out of sight, I walked as quietly as I could around the trailer, ducking under one window but heading toward the next one because I judged by the sound of their voices that it would be off to the side. Lord only knew what Curt would do if he saw me looking in.

Role reversal. Now I got to be the Peeping Tom. Crouching at the corner of the window, I inched upward enough so just one eye cleared the sill.

I could see pretty well by the light from the doorway, but it was hard to take in what I saw.

My sister, tied to a metal kitchen chair.

Blood on her silver-blond hair. Blood on her face. Blood on her clothes.

Not *her* clothes, really. Tiny black nightie kind of thing, sick sexy.

Her head drooping to one side. Her eyes closed.

Him. Crouching over her from behind. One skinny arm clenched around her chest.

The other hand pressing a knife to her throat.

A long, nasty-looking knife.

I put together most of this after I eased down and away from the window. One look, and I was too stunned, too afraid he'd notice me, so I pulled back and hunkered down a minute to study the picture in my mind.

"...might as well not *exist* as far as she's concerned," Curt was whining. "She stepped on my foot once in the hallway at school..."

I started sneaking back around the trailer toward the doorway.

"...didn't even bother to say she was *sorry*, didn't even notice, she doesn't even *remember*. I left flowers on her locker, and she threw them away. Every time..."

He sounded like he was pumping up his anger instead of getting rid of it. Feeding it like a fire, flames flickering into full blaze. Sounding more and more torqued as I reached the bottom of the three wooden steps.

I had to do something, and there was no time to think about it much. I got down flat on my stomach on the steps, hoping I could crawl up and he wouldn't see me.

He was ranting, "Every single time she was in a concert or a play or something I came hours early to get my seat, I was right there in the front row, but she never—"

"Of course!" Mom interrupted. "I thought you looked familiar. You're little Curtie Crocker!"

She sounded as if she was absolutely delighted to recognize an old friend in a strange place, and I knew that, being Mom, she was beaming like a lighthouse, which of course didn't make sense but it didn't have to. It fizzled his fire.

He squeaked, "Huh?"

"Little Curtie Crocker from Sumac! I remember you! You lived in that nice trailer park behind the sawmill. You liked to play with matches." She actually chuckled. "Got in trouble a couple of times that way, didn't you?"

By now I was lying on the platform outside the door, and I could see him gawking at Mom. His knife—I had to focus on him, compress my rage like plastic explosive, and hold it back— his knife had sagged like his jaw. Not really close to cutting Kari's throat anymore.

Staring at Mom with weird wistful disbelief, he croaked, "You really remember me?"

I pulled my feet under me in a crouch, holding on until—

"Of course I do! I knew your mother. Wasn't she a cashier in the Safeway? Linda Crocker?"

Curt's knife hand dropped almost to his knee.

Until the right time. Now.

I released my rage in an explosion of energy that burst from me in a werewolf yell as I rammed in.

ELEVEN

I had no strategy, no idea how to deal with the knife, no plan except to knock that bastard as far as possible from my sister. I'd never played football, but I tackled anyway, leading with my head and shoulders and giving everything I had to the impact. I hit hard between the creep and the chair my sister was tied to, knocking it to one side and shoving him back, his arms flailing. I didn't know whether he still had his knife, and I didn't care. I punched him as hard as I could and kept hitting, kicking—I can't give a blow-by-blow. Very confused, and all the time there was this background noise like a bad smell in the air. He fought, first trying to hurt me, then trying to get away from me, because I was crazy with an anger so strong I felt no pain and knew nothing except I was going to get him, get him, get him good. I think we clinched, and wrestled, and rolled on the floor. But the only thing I remember for sure is sitting on his back, pinning his arms behind him with one hand and punching,

punching his ugly ear. I remember because that's when a familiar voice cut through the background noise.

"Easy, Rig. You don't want to kill him."

My father. And I was so obsessed, I didn't even wonder how he'd got there. It just annoyed me, because I *did* want to kill the bastard.

Dad reached down with one of those white plastic sawtooth things meant for garbage bags, fastened it around the creep's wrists, and pulled it tight. He said, "Stay on top of him a minute," as he took off his belt—trust Dad to wear a belt—and wrapped it hard around the creep's ankles several times and cinched it like he was cinching a saddle onto a horse.

"Okay, that should do it." Dad gave me a hand up but didn't let go, because I couldn't seem to stand or balance. Too much to sort out. My rage seeping away, leaving me weak and, what was worse, starting to think again.

The stinking background noise. It was Curt cursing, whining, whimpering, yelling, swearing, trying to sound like a man.

My mother. I saw her crying without a sound. Tears running down her face. Yet moving efficiently, she used the knife, Curt's ugly knife, to cut the white plastic garbage ties that fastened my sister to the metal chair. A pile of them sat on the countertop. Dad had grabbed one, as good as a set of handcuffs on my sister's stalker.

My sister. Her eyes bruised and closed, her neck limp, her head hanging to one side. I started to shake all over. A horrible question rose in my throat and stuck there. Choking me.

Mom seemed to hear it anyway. "She's breathing," she said, her voice somehow calm even though tears dripped from her face, "and she has a pulse, pretty strong, I think. George, come help me get her on the couch."

I couldn't stop shaking. Dad leaned me against the kitchen counter, and I grabbed it and held on. He looked at me, and I nodded. I couldn't talk, but I'd be okay.

Bits and pieces again. Dad placed Karma's bare feet on the armrest of the couch. Why up there? He went farther into the trailer and came back with blankets and covered Kari with them. Mom sat with a pan of water and Dad's handkerchief—trust Dad to carry a real cloth handkerchief—dabbing at the blood on Kari's face, trying to uncover the damage without hurting her.

Curt, still on the floor, howling like an animal, thrashing, throwing a fit, using language so bad that Dad put duct tape over his mouth. Dad, both hands under the blankets, rubbing Karma's feet. Me, pushing off the kitchen counter and wobbling over to her, even though I felt shakier than ever. It scared me something awful to see Kari lying there like that, like she might be in a coma, like she might...die.

My voice came back in a cracked whisper. "We need an ambulance."

In a stretched-tight way, Dad said, "One of us has to go up to the top of the hill where there's a signal and call 911."

"Call 911," murmured Kari.

"Kari!" we all three exclaimed at once, and she opened her bruised eyes and stared through the slits.

She saw all of us, and she could have reached for Dad or me, we were both right there, but she cried, "Mommy!" and started to sob. She turned, head and shoulders in Mom's lap, Mom holding her—Kari, always Daddy's girl, crying like a baby in her mother's arms.

And me? Mom's little Riggie-Poo? For the first time in my life, I turned to my father and hung on to him, trembling, blubbering with relief that Kari was awake and it looked like she was going to be okay. I felt his big hand cradling my head against his shoulder, his strong arms around me. I felt his chest heave, heard the catch in his voice as he said, "Son, you found her. You saved your sister. I am proud of you, so proud of you I can't..." Then he stopped talking, and I felt something like a drop of rain fall on my hair.

It took a long time for the ambulance and the police to get there. So long that Creepo Curt actually wore himself out with his tantrum and lay still on the floor.

"What's taking them so long?" I complained at one point.

Dad, who had hiked up the hill to make the call, said, "They have to find the place."

Which reminded me. "How did *you* get here?"

"With difficulty."

He made me smile. "You know what I mean," I said. "How'd you know to come here?"

Piling logs into the woodstove to keep the fire going so Kari would be warm, he grinned at me. "I had expected to go along with Detective Steverson, so I was not pleased when he dumped me at the police station with nothing to do but listen to a scanner. Then I heard your call about smoke, and I don't know which bent me out of shape more, that you weren't resting like I told you to"—he gave me the funniest look—"or that Steverson wouldn't listen to you. I mean, sure, it was a long shot, but I hadn't heard any better ideas. So screw the cop bureaucracy. I went out smoke-hunting myself. Picked up a battery-operated scanner at Walmart so I could still listen in on the police. But I couldn't see any smoke, and I was just about to give up when I heard a report of some woman motorist stranded on a jeep track back in the hills. Knowing your mother, how she forgets to check the gas gauge"—Mom made a face at him from her seat by Kari's head—"I put two and two together and followed the GPS coordinates. Riggie, just relax. Give yourself a break."

Dad had fit me onto the couch, too, with my head beside Kari's feet, and he'd spread the blankets to cover me. Fussing over me. I didn't think I needed it, but I went along with it.

Dad went on with his story. "These roads make a can of fishing worms look straight, but finally I spotted the car. Didn't know what to think when I found it empty, so I got out, saw your tracks in the mud, followed them, found the trailer, and in I came just in time for the finale. You and your mother could have handled it without me."

"I'm certainly glad you're here," Mom said with unusual warmth—well, unusual when she was speaking to Dad.

I agreed. "So am I."

"But I didn't have to do anything. When I got here, you were sitting on top of the creep, walloping him, and Rosalie was busy with Kari."

We all looked at Kari, who tried to smile from her pillow. Her face was a mess. She was a mess. Alive, but a mess. Mom had said not to make her try to talk. So we were talking around her, like it was all about her but she wasn't there, and it felt wrong to me.

"Kari," I blurted, lifting myself up to look into her face, "did he rape you?"

"Ringgold!" Mom snapped, shocked.

Kari said, "No."

Oh, thank God. I felt a weight like a vulture fly off my chest.

"Riggie," Kari said slowly through bruised lips, "thank you."

"Huh?"

"For asking."

"Well, I thought he was going to rape you at least, even if he didn't kill you."

"Rig!" It was Dad this time.

"He was," Kari said. "Both of the above."

"Kari, relax, sweetie." Mom put a hand on her forehead. "Don't try to talk."

Kari ignored her. "But at first he was trying to pretend I was his own true love." She spoke straight to me. "Forget he snatched me from behind with a knife to my throat and dragged me down the hotel stairwell. Trying to believe I wanted to be here."

I nodded. "Roses?"

"Oh, yeah. In the bedroom. Soft music. Made me . . . undress."

Mom cried, "Kari, you don't need to tell us these things!"

Kari gave her a look like a left hook. "You don't want to hear, plug your ears."

"He made you get into that damn ridiculous slut outfit," I said. "What a total creep."

Kari nodded. "But I wouldn't kiss him. He slapped me. I tried to run. He caught me and tied me up."

"And beat on you."

"After a while. When I wouldn't agree. First he talked and talked...."

She really was getting tired. "Let me guess," I told her. "Why couldn't you see you were *his* girl, you had always belonged to him, you were meant to stay with him forever even if he had to kill you, that kind of thing?"

She nodded. "Riggie, how do you know?"

"Research," I said, but the truth was, somehow I was able to get inside Curt's head, and I wasn't about to say that. It wasn't a comfortable feeling. Made me wonder about myself.

I forced myself to say, "Finally he flipped out? Went psycho?"

"Oh, yeah." Kari closed her eyes. "Awful. Instead of just smacking me around, he started—"

Dad put in quietly, "We can try to imagine."

Kari gave a hint of a nod. "I guess he knocked me out. I woke up, and you all were here." Silent tears pooled around her swollen eyes. "Like a dream. Or a miracle."

"Or people who love you," Mom said.

"I'll second that," Dad said gruffly, "and now I agree with your mother you shouldn't try to talk. Riggie, you, either. You don't seem to realize how used up you are, son. Just lie still, relax. Your sister is going to be okay."

I guess those were the magic words, because I must have fallen asleep—well, I hadn't slept in a couple of days. I didn't even hear when the cops finally got there. I woke up when the medics moved me to take me to the hospital.

TWELVE

Kari and I ended up in the emergency room, but I didn't consider myself an emergency. I sat on the side of my cot and watched all the nurses and doctors and people in scrubs swarm around her. Between interns taking blood samples and techs taking X rays and cops taking her statement, it was pretty confusing for a while. The cops took my statement, too; and the docs took a look at me and my stab wounds, pulled the gauze out, put a couple of stitches in each cut, then said I could go. Dad wanted them to keep me overnight, but they said there was no medical reason, no significant new injuries. Apparently I'd knocked the knife out of Curt's hand when I'd rushed him, and Mom had grabbed it. They said the previous knife jabs were clear of infection, my pulse and blood pressure and everything were perfectly normal. I was a healthy, resilient teenage boy. Feed me and I'd be fine.

But then the cops wanted to talk with Mom and Dad, and, get this, they said the trailer where we'd found Kari was nowhere near that smoke Mom and I had spotted behind the campus. The roads had twisted us around so much that we ended up miles away from there. I couldn't believe it. But we took the elevator up to the top of the hospital to look, and that chalk line of smoke was still pointing to the wrong place—had to be the wrong place, because I knew we'd put out the fire in Curt's miserable trailer before we left.

I don't know why it was so hard for me to believe this, when it was also true that if the car hadn't run out of gas, we'd still be driving around totally lost, and Kari would still be—

Oh, God. Oh, Kari. After all my bright ideas, it was just dumb luck that we'd found her.

Just idiot luck.

"Except," Dad pointed out, "in order for it to happen, you had to be there."

"The Tao of Dad," I said.

"In my experience," Mom added serenely, "things just generally turn out all right."

"And the World According to Mom." I wished I could believe one of them. But it didn't matter. I had plenty of time to figure out the Rigmarole of Riggie.

After the cops left, we hung around the emergency room until the doctors finished with Kari. She had no broken bones, no serious injuries, but she did have a concussion, plus extensive bruising and lacerations, especially to her head. Her pulse was low, and they were worried she might go into shock. That was why Dad had elevated her feet and covered her with blankets, to prevent shock. Once in the hospital, she had started shaking with a delayed-reaction, irrational fear of Curt, even though he was in jail now. She was pale, clinging to Mom; the doctors said they wanted to keep her for observation.

So Mom stayed with Kari at the hospital and, sometime after dark, Dad and I went back to the hotel. Hospital security had kept reporters out of there, but news crews swarmed us at the hotel entrance, and while we were pushing our way through their microphones, they recorded pictures of me with my adorable broken nose. They followed us, so we couldn't eat in the hotel restaurant. We hid out in our room, and Dad phoned downstairs for Neapolitan ice cream, PBJ sandwiches on soft white bread, prime rib with mashed potatoes and asparagus, more mashed potatoes on the side, Gatorade with a straw, tropical fruit salad, a Bloody Mary, strawberry Jell-O. I had no problem guessing what was for him and what was for me.

Lying on my bed waiting for the food, I said, "After we eat I'm going to sleep until—What time is it and what day is it?"

"Around nine o'clock of the day you saved your sister's life."

His saying it that way, with wonder in his voice, should have made me feel good, but for some weird reason it made me real uncomfortable. I felt my face go hot, and I had to look away. Dad sat down on the side of my bed and studied me.

"Rig, is something bothering you?"

I hadn't felt so close to my dad in years. I muttered, "That creep."

"You trailed him almost single-handed."

I made myself look at my father. "Because I imagined—I kind of knew—he's so sick but—Dad, I understood him too well. What if I'm *like* him?"

Dad did not answer quickly. I watched him think awhile

before he said, "I need to deal with crooked businessmen some-times. And I understand them thoroughly. I have to. But that doesn't mean *I'm* crooked."

"It doesn't make you feel dirty?"

"Actually, sometimes it does. But I think this is a lot worse for you because it has to do with sex." The way I flinched when he said *sex* made me admit he was right. "Have you had a real girlfriend yet, Rig?"

I felt my face go red again. "No," I mumbled.

"But you're fifteen. You're basically just hormones on feet, so you think about it a lot."

"Every eight minutes on the average."

"Ow."

"Oh, yeah." Then I laid there expecting the obvious advice: to be responsible, respect girls, wait for someone who cared about me, and in general not be like Curt. But Dad totally surprised me.

He said, "To get inside this guy's head, you had to see your sister as sexually attractive. Is that what's bothering you, son?"

I guess it was, because my eyes shut hard and I stiffened like King Tut's mummy.

"Rig?"

I forced myself to open my eyes, look at him, and answer. "Photos of her boobs, photos of her butt, photos through the bedroom curtains; it was pretty hard to miss."

Dad sighed and nodded. "Which through no fault of yours got you tangled up in the world's oldest taboo: incest. But Rig, you recognize it, and you're dealing with it. You'll take care of it. Son, even when you didn't do what I said, you did everything right. You're a hero."

Hero?

When really I just got lucky?

But like Dad said, I had to be there.

He called me a hero. Wow. Now I go *wow*, but then all I said was, "I think of that creep, and I feel like slug slime."

"You got touched by slug slime, that's all." Dad looked sad. "And it's my fault you could ever think you're even remotely like that loser."

Dad? Fault? Saying so? I laid there with my mouth open, staring at him.

Facing me eye to eye, he told me, "I never realized how much I kept putting you down until you fought back." He winced, but he wouldn't look away. "It looks like I've caused you to have a low opinion of yourself, or you'd know how exceptional you are, the way you tracked that pervert."

I remember all this now and feel how wonderful it was, but at the time I just I wanted to lighten things up. I smiled and tried to joke. "Does this mean no more nagging me about my posture?"

It backfired. He looked like I'd jammed our mutual life history down his throat.

"Dad, it's okay. I don't mind," I lied. Then a thought struck me. "But listen, if you're impressed because I got into a couple of fights, I have to tell you, I don't plan on doing that as a regular thing."

So I'm serious, and he breaks up laughing. I may never figure out my parents. By the time he'd finished laughing, he'd relaxed, and I could see he was okay again. "There's one of your sterling qualities," he told me. "Your flabbergasting honesty."

"Flabbergasting?"

At which point the food arrived, thank goodness. And I didn't hesitate to reach for the ice cream first. I figured I'd earned it.

Fast forward a few months.

One thing is, the first time I got a chance to talk to my mom, I told her how well she'd handled Curt at the trailer. She said, "He had Kari, I had to distract him, and I did what I do best." Yes, she really did remember "little Curtie" from Sumac, and he was a mess even as a kid. He set fires. He was cruel to animals. He was always getting kicked out of school. He was an only child, with no dad, and his mother wasn't the brightest spoon in the drawer. She totally spoiled him, like, the axis of the universe was Curtie as far as his mommy was concerned. No wonder he grew up thinking he could have whatever he wanted, and he was entitled to take it.

He was a high school dropout, a loser, a psycho, and a criminal.

I wasn't much like him after all.

Another thing is, when I went back to school, forget the cliques that had already clicked. Partly because Kari needed to be in the city with Mom, and partly because Dad and I wanted to give each other a chance, I was living with him, going to Sumac High School, and liking it a lot. Back in Sumac, no way was I a loner anymore. To my amazement, kids remembered me from four years ago and welcomed me back. I had instant friends and then some, because I joined the art club to test whether my new-and-improved father was for real, and the debate club to hone my skills of arguing with him in case he reverted to type.

Dad still called me Big Rig all the time, but now he wasn't being sarcastic. He meant it, so I liked it. He didn't put me down too much anymore, except sometimes he grumbled about my hair or my shoes or kidded me about finding a girlfriend, but no problem; I could handle it. I could stand up to him now, and he knew it. Most of the time we got along, actually talking and doing things together, like cooking some pretty strange suppers.

I phoned Mom and Karma just about every day. Kari had taken time off from college to see a counselor and do art and take tae kwon do lessons and generally deal with the aftermath. (Or, as Mom would say, "Enjoy all the advantages the city has to offer.")

Even though Curt was still in jail—we kept track of him; he couldn't make bail—even though she'd escaped her stalker without too much physical damage, Kari still had emotional damage to work through. For the time being Curt had stolen her self-confidence, her sense of security.

She wasn't looking forward to testifying at the creep's trial. If there was a trial. He might just plead no contest because the prosecution had a strong case. But on the other hand, maybe Curt was crazy enough to want his day in court. I hoped Kari wouldn't have to go through that, but she had told me that trial or no trial, she was going to be okay. It was just going to take some time.

Funny how it wasn't hard to talk with her anymore. Most evenings I would get on the phone to say hi to Mom then yak with my sister.

"Are you okay with Mom?" I asked Kari after the first couple of weeks. "I mean, is she living on the same planet with you?"

"Not really. But that's okay. Mom is Mom. She handles things her way, and I handle them my way."

"Yeah, well, how's therapy?"

"Nunya," Kari said, meaning "private and none of your business." But then she went on, "Riggie, do you ever think or, like, dream that our parents could get back together?"

"The standard kids' postdivorce fantasy in which Mommy and Daddy still wuv each other?"

"That's the one."

"Oh, yeah. Wish Fulfillment R Us. I go there."

"Do you think it could ever really happen?"

"When Dad learns to appreciate Picasso, and pigs fly."

She laughed her unmistakable laugh, the color of her hair. "I knew I could count on you, Rig. Thank you."

I had no idea what she was thanking me for or why I said what I did next, except I felt like she needed to hear it. And I'd never said it before. But I do know for sure that it had nothing to do with slug slime when I told her, "I love you."

And she shot back happily, "Duh, Big Rig, I never would have guessed."